Outstanding praise for the novels of Holly Chamberlin!

THE SEASON OF US

"A warm and witty tale. This heartfelt and emotional story will appeal to members of the Sandwich Generation or anyone who has had to set aside long-buried childhood resentments for the well-being of an aging parent. Fans of Elin Hilderbrand and Wendy Wax will adore this genuine exploration of family bonds, personal growth, and acceptance."
—*Booklist*

"Chamberlin successfully portrays a family at their best and worst as they struggle through their first holiday without a beloved husband and father and have to redefine their relationships."
—*Library Journal*

THE BEACH QUILT

"Particularly compelling."
—*The Pilot*

SUMMER FRIENDS

"A thoughtful novel."
—*ShelfAwareness*

"A great summer read."
—*Fresh Fiction*

"A novel rich in drama and insights into what factors bring people together and, just as fatefully, tear them apart."
—*The Portland Press Herald*

THE FAMILY BEACH HOUSE

"Explores questions about the meaning of home, family dynamics and tolerance."
—*The Bangor Daily News*

"An enjoyable summer read, but it's more. It is a novel for all seasons that adds to the enduring excitement of Ogunquit."
—*The Maine Sunday Telegram*

"It does the trick as a beach book and provides a touristy taste of Maine's seasonal attractions."
—*Publishers Weekly*

Books by Holly Chamberlin

LIVING SINGLE

THE SUMMER OF US

BABYLAND

BACK IN THE GAME

THE FRIENDS WE KEEP

TUSCAN HOLIDAY

ONE WEEK IN DECEMBER

THE FAMILY BEACH HOUSE

SUMMER FRIENDS

LAST SUMMER

THE SUMMER EVERYTHING CHANGED

THE BEACH QUILT

SUMMER WITH MY SISTERS

SEASHELL SEASON

THE SEASON OF US

HOME FOR THE SUMMER

HOME FOR CHRISTMAS

Published by Kensington Publishing Corporation

The Season of Us

Holly Chamberlin

KENSINGTON BOOKS
http://www.kensingtonbooks.com

KENSINGTON BOOKS are published by

Kensington Publishing Corp.
119 West 40th Street
New York, NY 10018

All Kensington titles, imprints and distributed lines are available at special quantity discounts for bulk purchases for sales promotion, premiums, fund-raising, educational or institutional use.

Special book excerpts or customized printings can also be created to fit specific needs. For details, write or phone the office of the Kensington Special Sales Manager: Kensington Publishing Corp., 119 West 40th Street, New York, NY 10018, Attn. Special Sales Department. Phone: 1-800-221-2647.

Kensington and the K logo Reg. U.S. Pat. & TM Off.

First Kensington Hardcover Edition: November 2016
ISBN-13: 978-1-4967-0682-9
ISBN-10: 1-4967-0682-X
First Kensington Trade Paperback Edition: October 2017

eISBN-13: 978-1-4967-0683-6
eISBN-10: 1-4967-0683-8
First Kensington Electronic Edition: November 2016

10 9 8 7 6 5 4 3 2

Printed in the United States of America

As always, for Stephen
And this time, also for Joe and Rusty Donner

Acknowledgments

There would be no Holly Chamberlin without John Scognamiglio, so once again, my most sincere gratitude. And to my family—parents, grandparents, aunt and uncles—I offer many thanks for making Christmas a magical time for my brother and me when we were young.

*Love begins by taking care of the closest ones—
the ones at home.*

—Mother Teresa

The Season of Us

CHAPTER 1

Gincy stood at the windows in the living area of the Leather District loft she shared with her family. The people who lived in the loft directly across from theirs were lucky enough to have a covered deck, and on it they had arranged a row of four potted trees, each beautifully decorated. There was the angel tree, replete with ethereal winged creatures carrying elaborate lanterns and blowing on golden trumpets. Next to it stood the Santa tree, adorned with charming figurines representing the changing image of St. Nicholas over the centuries. The third tree, Gincy's favorite, was trimmed with gorgeously colored glass birds, from iridescent blue and green peacocks to scarlet cardinals to shimmering white swans. And the fourth tree was entirely covered in bows made of pale pink and powder blue velvet.

That was one of the wonderful things about living in Boston, Gincy thought as she turned away from the windows. There was always something interesting around the next corner—or, in this case, out of your window—especially at the holiday season.

And it *was* the holiday season, with Christmas about a

week away, and then, a week after that, the start of a new year. The truth was that Gincy wouldn't be sad to see the old year go.

Certainly, there had been good times. In early August she and her husband, Rick, and their two children, Justin and Tamsin, had spent a week on Martha's Vineyard in a charming cottage blissfully situated in the middle of nowhere. Back in early June, Tamsin had ended her freshman year of high school with honors, and Justin received an unexpected promotion at work. And Gincy and Rick had managed a romantic autumn getaway weekend in Quebec City.

But the year had brought with it trying times, too. Worst of all, Gincy's beloved father had died at the beginning of June, slipping away in his sleep at the age of seventy-eight. Rick had pointed out that Ed Gannon's manner of passing was a sort of blessing. He hadn't suffered. He hadn't had to endure a long and painful illness, sparing Ellen Gannon, Ed's wife of over fifty years, the financial devastation a prolonged illness might have wrought, not to mention the emotional strain.

That was all true. Still, the fact was that her father was gone, and six months after his death Gincy was still grieving, though with every passing day there came a greater degree of peace and acceptance. And because she and her father had grown so much closer over time, she felt little in the way of regret or lost opportunity. It had taken her almost thirty years to open her eyes and look closely at the man she had always loved uncomplicatedly as Dad and to finally see the whole person, the individual man of sensitivity and talents she had never really noticed. She had taken her father for granted, she felt, and so on the cusp of her thirtieth birthday she had set about making reparations by inviting him to visit her in Boston; introducing him to Rick and Justin; going for long, slow walks to-

gether; asking his opinions; learning more about his childhood and what really made him laugh; discovering his favorite
foods, the long-remembered dishes his mother had cooked for
her family that Ellen Gannon did not care to cook for hers.
The revitalized relationship with her father had brought
Gincy so much happiness, and, she believed, it had done
the same for her father.

And now that he was gone, Gincy was getting on with
life in the way she always had. Since she was a little girl
she had been known as the strong, no-nonsense one people
turned to in a crisis—as long as the crisis didn't include anything *too* emotionally demanding. Being warm and fuzzy
was sometimes a challenge for her, except when it came to
her children and her husband. She was unabashedly emotional with the three of them and had embarrassed the
kids, if not Rick, time and again with public displays of
love and pride.

Tamsin: "Mom, did you have to scream so loud when I
scored that goal? Everybody was looking at you."

Justin: "Mom, please don't hug and kiss me so much in
front of my friends."

Gincy was working from home that afternoon, something she didn't do often, but there were moments—and
they came more frequently these days—when she needed
the utter quiet of her home in order to properly think, edit,
and write.

After graduation from Addison College with a degree in
communications, Gincy had taken a lowly job as an assistant's assistant at one of Boston's public broadcasting sta-
tions. Making rent was a challenge for the first few years
of her professional life, let alone keeping herself in decent
clothing, but she had soldiered on, rising steadily until at
the age of twenty-nine she was appointed senior editor of
the station's monthly print publication.

Now, after a journey that included a few years as an in-house writer for a magazine dedicated to the visual arts (the magazine had never been profitable and had finally run out of operating funds) and a brief stint as the editor of a society column for a women's glossy (she had never been able to work up interest in who wore what when and where), she was a senior editor-at-large at the *Globe*, the city's most respected newspaper. It was a job she had earned, and she loved everything about it.

When Gincy or Rick worked from home, they set up at the dining table, Gincy at one end and Rick at the other. Though she worked on a laptop for final copy, she still used a yellow legal pad and pencil to make a good deal of her notes. And not a mechanical pencil either, but the kind with lead you had to sharpen with one of those little plastic-covered blade thingies. Her daughter, who did all of her homework on her computer, found this intensely amusing.

Gincy glanced back at the beautifully decorated trees across the way and not for the first time realized just how happy she was living where she did. They had bought the loft ten years earlier; it had been in decent condition and had required little repair or updating. Most of the twenty-two-hundred feet of living space was on the lower level; only Rick and Gincy's bedroom and bathroom were on the second level. There were several exposed brick walls, a wonderfully high ceiling, and hardwood floors through-out. Large windows provided lots of natural light.

Justin, now twenty-five and Rick's son from his first marriage, lived in Greenwich, Connecticut. He still kept a fair amount of his "stuff" in his old room, though he rarely visited. Except for the week on the Vineyard, the family had not seen him since his grandfather's funeral. To his credit he kept in regular touch through e-mail and the occasional phone call.

Tamsin, Gincy's fifteen-year-old daughter with Rick, was a bright and good-natured young woman. Still, for all of that she was a notorious slob, and her bedroom was best entered with caution. She was personally clean—Tamsin spent a big part of her allowance on organic soaps, shampoos, and body lotions—but the notion of putting dirty clothes into the laundry hamper instead of on the floor and making her bed on any regular basis seemed not to interest her.

It wasn't rebellion. Gincy recognized teenaged rebellion when she saw it. Tamsin just didn't *think* about order and neatness. Gincy hadn't thought about such things either when she was young; in college her roommate had nicknamed her Moldy, and the nickname had not been entirely unfair.

Gincy looked at her watch. It was almost three o'clock, time for her afternoon pick-me-up. She went to the kitchen and poured what was left of the breakfast coffee into a mug, heated it in the microwave, and took it back to the dining table where she sat in one of the two ergonomic chairs Rick had insisted they buy. "It's a waste of money," she had protested, but in fact the chairs were insanely comfortable, and more than once she had found herself nodding off in one of them when she should have been paying bills.

Before opening the file she had been working on earlier, Gincy checked her personal e-mail account and found no fewer than eleven announcements of Once in a Lifetime Holiday Sales that Absolutely Could Not Be Missed. She deleted all of them. She had completed her Christmas shopping and decorating the week before; her cards had gone out the second week of the month. Gincy was nothing if not organized, and she had never, ever missed a deadline of any sort.

Along the shelf behind the couch she had set out twelve white candles in an eclectic selection of candlesticks collected from sidewalk sales and antique shops. Four bright red felt stockings already bulging with small treats, hung from the shelf. Justin's train set—a vintage model Rick had found at an estate sale in Portland—curled around the base of the tree, a fresh blue spruce Gincy watered twice a day. You could never be too careful. It was something her father used to say about pretty much everything he thought might be a potential hazard, from dry Christmas trees to sharp edges on the lids of metal cans.

The tree was hung with simple glass ornaments in blue and red, but there were also ornaments with more personal meaning, like the tiny ceramic angels Tamsin had been collecting for the past few years and miniatures of the characters from Justin's all-time favorite Christmas special, *Rudolph the Red-Nosed Reindeer*. At the very top of the tree sat a large silvery star.

To complete the holiday décor, Tamsin had hung a red metal jingle bell on the front door. It made a horrible clanging racket every time the door was opened or closed, but she loved it and the neighbors hadn't complained so there it stayed.

A few presents were already gathered under the tree, including a small box wrapped in gold paper and tied with a red velvet ribbon. Gincy knew what Rick was giving her for Christmas—a brown leather blazer to replace the one she had been wearing for fifteen years—and as an article of clothing would never fit in a box that measured only about three square inches, it was a safe assumption that the little box contained something special to mark the occasion of her fiftieth birthday on the first of January. And she was pretty sure she knew what it was.

The last time she and Rick had spent the day in Portsmouth they had wandered into Market Square Jewelers, a store that offered an incredible selection of vintage and antique items. Almost immediately, a small gold fede— "faith" or "fidelity"—ring dating from the Georgian period had caught her eye. The symbolism of two hands clasped was simple but powerful, and she had remarked on it. It would be just like Rick to buy her the ring for a landmark birthday.

Sheesh, she thought, closing the e-mail program and opening the file on which she had been working earlier. *Half a century on this planet.* She had been told often enough that she "didn't look her age," which she supposed meant that she didn't look like a total physical wreck. Still, her short dark hair was threaded with a few gray strands, and she had started to carry a pair of reading glasses in her bag. And she was no longer the scrawny thing that Rick had first met and fallen in love with. Time, having a baby, and living with a man who liked to keep her well fed had seen to that.

Gincy's cell phone rang just as she took the first sip of her coffee. She pulled the phone from the pocket of her wool sweater and recognized the New Hampshire area code. But it was not her mother's number, and the only other person she knew in the state was her brother and he never called her. They were not the kind of siblings who kept in regular touch; they had absolutely nothing in common except a bit of shared DNA.

If this was Tommy, no good could come of whatever her ne'er-do-well brother was calling about. Of that she was sure. The last time Tommy had called out of the blue, it was from the emergency room one town over from Appleville. He had totaled a friend's car—not that it was his fault—and the thing was his friend had said he could borrow the car but now he was saying Tommy had taken it without permission and that he was going to report Tommy to the police and could Gincy tell him what he should do. Oh, and he had a broken wrist and could Gincy not tell Mom and Dad what had happened. And the time before that . . .

"Hello?" she said, answering the call with a frown.

"Gince, it's me. Tommy. Your brother. Oh, right. You know that. Look, I need help with Mom."

"What do you mean *help*?" Gincy asked. *He's going to ask for money again,* she thought. Nothing ever changed with Tommy. There were three things you could count on in this world. Death. Taxes. And Tommy never changing.

"Something's wrong," he said. "The other night I was over at Mom's house for dinner and the potatoes were, like, half cooked. And she didn't even notice. And the milk had gone sour. You know how crazy she is about milk being fresh. The second she thinks it's going off, bam, right down the sink."

What's the big deal about half-cooked potatoes or sour milk? Gincy thought. Neither seemed to warrant this call for help from her brother. "I'm not sure what you're getting at," she said.

"And there's kind of a musty smell in the upstairs hallway."

Gincy resisted rolling her eyes. "Did you try opening a few windows in the rooms along the hall to let in some fresh air?"

"Oh," Tommy said. "No. But the worst thing is that the electric company turned off Mom's lights just because she forgot to pay last month's bill. I mean, how can they do that to an old lady?"

Gincy sighed. "That's not how it works, Tommy. Look, did she eventually pay the bill? Does she have power back?"

"Yeah. But I think it freaked her out. I mean, she didn't

say that she was freaked out, but I could tell. She never forgets stuff."

He was right about that, Gincy thought. Her mother had a mind like a steel trap when it came to things like paying bills and balancing her budget. "Did she actually tell you she forgot to pay the bill?" she asked. "How did you find out?"

"I went over there one morning and she was upset that the toaster wasn't working and that the coffeepot wasn't perking or whatever and she said that a bunch of light-bulbs had burned out overnight and I said, That's weird, maybe you forgot to pay the electric bill. I meant it as a joke but she went all white and that's what it was, she'd forgotten."

Gincy wondered what other bills her mother might have neglected to pay. Worse, she wondered what money Ellen might have been conned into giving away to some bogus charity or stranded African prince. It happened all the time. There was always someone around pathetic and im-moral enough to bilk the elderly. The situation could, in fact, be serious.

"Okay, Tommy," she said. "I'll call her this evening, though I'm not sure what I'll be able to find out."

"Thanks, Gince," Tommy said. "Look, don't tell her I called, okay? She made me promise not to tell you about the electric bill but . . ."

"Don't worry, Tommy. I won't say a word."

"Thanks again, Gince," he said, and Gincy could hear the unmistakable relief in his voice. "I owe you one."

It was no good. An hour after the disturbing call from her brother, Gincy still couldn't concentrate on correcting grammar and tightening sentence structure. Her conscience, that annoyingly vigilant thing, was bothering her.

The fact was that she had not been back to Appleville

since her father's funeral. And apart from her usual biweekly call to her mother and an obligatory call on Thanksgiving, she had had no further correspondence with her. Come to think of it, Gincy realized, Ellen hadn't sent them a card at Thanksgiving. That was odd. Maybe her mother, always frugal, had simply committed to further belt tightening now that her husband was gone. Or maybe sending a Thanksgiving card was something else that had slipped her mind.

And as for her brother . . . The last time Gincy had spoken to Tommy was during the course of their father's funeral, and that communication had been limited to her asking questions like, "Who was that man sitting two rows behind us at the wake, the one with the plaid jacket and bad toupee?" to which Tommy had replied with a shrug. Limited communication wasn't unusual for the Gannon siblings. Most every time Gincy did engage with her brother, she was left feeling frustrated, annoyed, or downright angry. He just never seemed to *listen*, and when he did listen he turned everything into a joke or he dismissed what she was saying with a grin and a shrug, even when a more appropriate answer might be "Thanks, Gincy, for asking about my friend's chemotherapy" or "Hey, Gincy, that's great news about the new job." When possible, she avoided conversation with people who routinely provoked such unpleasant feelings in her.

But now, at the distance of half a year, she remembered that at their father's funeral Tommy had seemed . . . What was it? Lost? Scared?

At the time she hadn't given his state of mind any thought. First there had been the wake to survive, two interminable three-hour viewings a day for two days straight, during which time she and her mother had shaken hands with what seemed like hundreds of sympathetic well-wishers.

Then had come the funeral at the church her mother had taken to frequenting in the last few years, followed by a visit to the cemetery, where at her father's grave the assistant pastor of the church had spoken a few additional words of comfort. Gincy had been too wrapped up in her own feelings of sadness and loss, too concerned with her role as her mother's representative with the funeral director, and too focused on giving what comfort she could to her children to pay any attention to her brother.

Thomas Edward Gannon, now forty-five years of age. For the past decade he had lived in a tiny apartment in an aluminum-sided house in the run-down section of Appleville, the owners of which hadn't bothered to mow the miniscule lawn or to replace several torn screens in the town's memory. Gincy had been to the apartment only once, and not because she was invited but because one of the other tenants had called the Gannons to say that he was hearing weird noises and smelling strange odors coming from Tommy's apartment. Gincy and Rick had been paying a flying visit to her parents on their way to Maine for a weekend. and rather than subject the Gannons to whatever unpleasantness they were bound to find at Tommy's home, they had driven to Birch Lane, fully expecting disaster.

But what they had found was innocuous enough. After a few minutes of loud knocking, the weird sounds stopped—electronic squeaks and squeals, interspersed with a screaming electric guitar—and Tommy had opened the door, rubbing his eyes and looking mildly puzzled. "Hey," he said. "Dudes, what are you doing here?" They had explained about the call from the concerned neighbor, at which point Tommy had burst out laughing. "Oh, man, Luke's so neurotic! He watches way too many cop shows."

Rick then asked about the sounds and the smell—more

pungent now that the door was open. The sounds had come from a CD put out by a local band. "They do experimental heavy metal stuff," Tommy had explained. The smell was coming from a batch of incense Tommy's girlfriend of the moment had made especially for him. "And why didn't you answer the door right away?" Gincy had demanded. Tommy had just shrugged.

Tommy had been married once for about a nanosecond. Well, six months, really. That's how long it had taken his poor wife to realize her mistake and contact a lawyer. He had no kids that he knew of. Gincy remembered his proclaiming that with a hearty laugh, but that had been years ago. Maybe now her brother took the idea of fatherhood more seriously. She wouldn't know. He was often out of work; Gincy had no idea how he paid his rent. He often couldn't afford to keep a car and routinely had to bum rides from friends. Back at Ed Gannon's funeral, he was in possession of a rusty old truck; Gincy suspected it had fallen apart by now.

But the most frustrating thing about Tommy was his attitude of entitlement and his irresponsibility. Nothing was ever his fault. The world was always against him and had been from the start. Gincy had lost track of the number of times she had heard him say something like, "If only I had some money, everything would be okay. I could really turn things around if only someone would give me a chance."

To be fair, Gincy thought, taking a sip of the now cold and muddy coffee, maybe Tommy didn't feel entitled. Maybe what was behind his view of the world and his place in it was a regrettable ignorance. That or a sense of his own inadequacy, something he could handle only by a big dose of wishful thinking. If that were the case, you could feel sorry for Tommy Gannon.

The second most frustrating thing about Tommy, at

least for his sister, was her mother's attitude toward him. Ellen Gannon saw her son through rose-colored glasses. Every conversation Gincy had ever had with her mother about Tommy followed pretty much the same script.

Mrs. Gannon: "Your poor brother has had terrible luck in life."

Gincy: "You make your own luck in this world, Mom. He doesn't even try."

Mrs. Gannon: "No woman has ever understood poor Tommy. Look at that woman he married. She was just a cold fish, leaving him like that. Heartless."

Gincy: "Mom, Tommy gambled away all of their money—not that there was much of it—within months of the wedding. And then he cheated on her with her best friend."

Mrs. Gannon: "You've always been too harsh on your little brother, Virginia."

Well, Gincy thought now, leaning back in her comfortable chair and remembering how lost or sad Tommy had seemed at Ed Gannon's funeral, yes, maybe she *had* been too harsh. But it was hard to place faith in someone who always let you down, even if he couldn't help but let you down because he didn't have the courage or the intelligence or the strength to do otherwise. Again, to be fair—something Gincy always tried to be though she failed more often than she would care to admit—her brother hadn't actually asked her for money since about two years back. But what did that mean, she wondered. That he was making enough money selling drugs or stealing from unattended cash registers to support himself?

Gincy felt her blood pressure rising. She would definitely wait until she talked to Rick about Tommy's phone call before getting in touch with Ellen and saying something she would regret. Rick was the rational one in the family. He could calm her down when she got worked up about her mother or her brother. Calming her down when she got worked up about her family—or about anything else—was only one of Rick Luongo's many, many good points.

CHAPTER 2

"Did you hear about the big accident on Storrow Drive this morning?" Rick asked, tossing a handful of chopped garlic into a saucepan.

"I did," Gincy said. "It's a miracle that no one was badly hurt. Something's got to be done about that section of road. It's a menace. I guess I'll have to write to our city councilor again. Or convince the paper to run another story about it."

Rick smiled. "That's one of the things I like about you, Gincy. You're not the type to complain about a situation and then do nothing about it."

"It's gotten me in trouble on occasion, hasn't it?"

"Only on occasion."

"Like the time I tried to intervene when I saw that disgusting man yanking his little girl's arm. He had her in a death grip, Rick, and right in the middle of the sidewalk. She was crying. What was I supposed to do, just keep walking?"

"No," Rick said carefully, "but in a situation like that, when violence is already happening, it might be wiser to call the police instead of launching yourself into the fray."

Gincy frowned at her husband. "Maybe."

At fifty-six, Rick Luongo was still fit, and his olive complexion and thick dark wavy hair still excited Gincy. It was always fun when she happened to catch sight of him on the street and think, "Now *there's* a good-looking guy," and then to realize a split second later that the good-looking guy was her own husband.

The two had met back when Rick had come to work as director of daytime programming at the public broadcasting station where Gincy was employed. On his very first day Gincy had spied him eating a jelly donut, oblivious to a great blob of jelly landing on his tie. The tie was printed with images of puppies; it was awful but adorable in its awfulness. She had been immediately drawn to someone who she sensed was completely unself-conscious and unashamedly who he was. Seriously, how many people had the courage to eat a jelly donut in public on the first day at an important job? The fact that on their first date she learned that he, too, hated anchovies and loved the works of Hunter S. Thompson had pretty much sealed the deal, though it had taken her the entire summer to work up the courage to make a real commitment to him.

It was the best decision she had ever made.

Currently Rick oversaw both the director of daytime and the director of nighttime programming at the station. The fact that he had been with the same company for twenty years made him a bit of a celebrity in the office. He had survived cutbacks and avoided dangerous personality disputes and unpleasant political coups and had continued to rise in place and esteem. At fifty-six, he found himself in the position of the respected and admired Grand Old Man.

While Rick continued to prepare dinner—a stir-fry with calamari, vegetables, and plenty of garlic and ginger—Gincy set three places at the large kitchen island.

"I got a call from Tommy today," she said.

Rick looked over his shoulder. "Really? That's pretty unusual. What did he have to say?"

"He said that Mom isn't doing so well. She forgot to pay the electric bill last month. The house smells musty. The milk went sour and she didn't notice. I have to say, Rick, I'm a bit worried. I'm going to call her this evening."

"Good," Rick said. "From what I've seen over the years, Tommy's not exactly an alarmist, nor is he the most perceptive fellow. If he thinks something is wrong, then it probably is."

"I know. It's just that . . ."

"Just that what?" Rick asked.

"Never mind." How could she admit, even to her husband, the person who knew and understood her best, that along with feeling genuine concern for her mother she was also feeling just a little bit annoyed? It was the Christmas season, the first one without her father, and she knew it was going to be difficult at moments, remembering all the good times they had shared, and she just hadn't *expected* a potential crisis with her mother on top of that emotional strain.

But life was never *expected*, was it? To survive, you had to adapt. Ed Gannon had always said as much.

"Mom told Tommy not to tell me about the electric bill," Gincy told her husband. "What do you think that's about?"

Rick shrugged. "She's embarrassed. You know how proud your mother is. Look, Gincy, you're sure you didn't pick up on something wrong the last time you talked to her?"

"No," Gincy said, turning away from her husband. "I didn't."

The clanging jingle bell announced that their daughter

was home, and a moment later Tamsin joined them in the kitchen, shedding winter garments as she went.

"Brrr, it's cold out there!" she announced as she kissed first her mother's cheek and then her father's.

"How was ice-skating?" Gincy asked, retrieving a purple mitten from the floor.

"Totally fun. I mean, I fell like three times. but no big deal. Julie fell five times!"

Rick sighed. "Ah, to be young enough to bounce up from a fall on the ice."

"I didn't exactly bounce, Dad. I kind of crawled up. That smells awesome. What are we having?"

Tamsin was, like both of her parents, about medium height, though possibly still growing. She had dark hair and was very thin, as her mother had been at that age. In terms of her personality, she was definitely more like her father, and Gincy was glad about that. Rick was pleasant. He was reasonable. He was everybody's friend. Gincy was prickly, though less so than she had been in her youth. She was not always reasonable. And she was not everybody's friend, nor did she wish to be.

Over second helpings of stir-fried calamari, vegetables, and jasmine rice, Gincy told Tamsin about her uncle's call. She and Rick weren't in the habit of keeping potentially difficult situations from their children. They felt it was better to be aware than to be in ignorance. Ignorance was not bliss; it was ignorance.

"Poor Grandma," Tamsin said. "She probably misses Grandpa so much."

"We don't know if whatever's going on with Grandma has anything to do with Grandpa," Gincy pointed out.

"Of course it does," Tamsin said. "She misses him so much that she's forgetting things. You get confused when you're sad. At least, I always do."

Mom just misses having someone around to criticize, Gincy thought. Really, she didn't know how her father had put up with it all those years. If the Gannons were Catholic, she would nominate her father for sainthood, not that she had the least idea of how to go about doing that.

"Justin is coming home for Christmas, I hope," Gincy said. It was time to change the subject. Talking about her mother could ruin her appetite, and she took her appetite seriously, especially when Rick had done the cooking.

Rick nodded. "He'll let us know exactly when in a day or two. He's shooting for the twenty-third, but it depends on the job."

The job, Gincy thought. It was more than just a job, and Justin had the MBA to prove it. He worked for a private equity group, and the fact that neither of his parents really understood what it was he did didn't matter, because Justin *did* understand. To say that she was proud of her stepson would be a vast understatement. Not that she found his taste in girlfriends all that wonderful, but maybe that was just the overprotective mother in her.

"Is he still seeing that girl, what's her name, the one with the nose ring?" Gincy asked.

"It's called a septum piercing, Mom. And no, they broke up."

"Good. I wasn't looking forward to having a daughter-in-law with a nose ring."

"A septum piercing."

"Whatever it's called, it's disgusting."

Tamsin rolled her eyes. "Mom, haven't you ever heard of live and let live?"

"Sure. She's free to have a nose ring. And I'm free to find it disgusting."

Rick shrugged. "Your mother has a point," he said.

"Not that I would ever tell Justin that I found something about his girlfriend physically objectionable," Gincy hastened to add. "I've spent a good part of my adult life preaching to anyone who will listen that looks mean nothing when judging a person's character."

Tamsin laughed. "And you wouldn't want Justin to think you were a hypocrite, right, Mom?"

"Right. And if the nose ring doesn't bother *him*, then it's none of my business."

Tamsin was right, Gincy thought, stabbing a piece of calamari and popping it into her mouth. The last thing she wanted to appear to either of her children was a hypocrite, but especially to her stepson, who had taken such a courageous chance in welcoming her into his life. She would never forget how nervous she had been meeting Justin for the first time all those years ago. But the little boy, who had no memory of the mother who had died so soon after his birth, had actually *liked* her. She remembered thinking that he must have been born with some sort of antinegativity shield. She could be grouchy and awkward when she was younger, but Justin, like his father, had been able to see through the scruffy exterior to the decent person inside.

"Why did they break up?" Gincy asked now. "Justin and The Nose Ring?"

"Her name is Lisa, Mom. Anyway, Justin told me Lisa complained that he spent too much time at work and that she felt ignored. So he had to end things. He told her he was sorry but he wasn't in love with her and that he had a career to build, and then he told *me* that someday, when he *is* in love, he'll spend less time working and more with the girlfriend, but not until then."

Gincy nodded. "That's our boy," she said. "He's got his priorities right. Wait, when did he tell you all this?"

Tamsin screwed up her face in thought. "Like, maybe a week ago?"

"And you didn't tell us before now?" Rick asked.

Tamsin shrugged. "I guess I forgot. Hey, Mom? I can't find my Chuck Taylor, the left one. No, it's the right one. Have you seen it?"

"Have you checked the fridge?"

"Ha, ha." And then Tamsin frowned. "Wait. Do you really think it could be in the fridge?"

Gincy laughed. "No, I don't," she said. "But I'll help you find it after dinner."

CHAPTER 3

At eight that evening, Gincy grit her teeth and called her mother. Mrs. Gannon answered after four rings of the landline.

"Mom," Gincy said. "It's me."

"Who?" Mrs. Gannon asked. Her voice sounded weak.

She's not being difficult, Gincy realized with some surprise. *She really doesn't know who I am.*

"It's Gincy, Mom," she said, a bit more loudly in case her mother simply hadn't heard her the first time.

"Oh," Mrs. Gannon said. "Hello, Virginia. Why are you calling? Has something happened? Is Tamsin all right?"

Gincy couldn't miss the note of real anxiety in her mother's voice. She couldn't remember ever hearing it before, not even when Tommy was arrested for petty theft back when he was sixteen. "Everything's okay, Mom," she said. "Nothing's happened. We're all doing well. I just thought I'd call."

"Oh."

"How are you, Mom?" Gincy asked. "Is everything okay there?"

"Everything is fine," Mrs. Gannon said. "Though . . ."

"Though what, Mom?"

"The roof could use fixing. I think. At least that's what your father said, and he handled all of those things. . . . But I just don't know."

"Is there a leak, Mom?" Gincy asked. "Is water coming through the ceiling anywhere?" Tommy hadn't said anything about a leaking roof, but maybe he simply didn't know about it.

"Has something happened?" Ellen asked again, ignoring Gincy's question, her voice quavering. "Is Tamsin hurt? Is it Justin?"

Gincy took a deep breath. Something was definitely, seriously wrong. Tommy had been right to call her. "Everyone is fine, Mom," she said in what she hoped was a reassuring voice. "I'm sorry to have called so late. Why don't we talk again tomorrow, all right?"

"Yes, Virginia, all right. Good-bye."

And Ellen Gannon hung up before her daughter could also say a farewell.

Gincy immediately called Tommy on his cell phone. He answered right away, as if he had been waiting for her call.

"Gince? What did she say?" Tommy asked.

"She said exactly what I expected her to say, that everything is fine. Of course, I don't believe her. Look, I'm coming up tomorrow," she told him. "But don't say anything to Mom."

"Why not?" Tommy asked.

"Just don't, please, Tommy."

"Okay."

"And Tommy?" she said. "Do you know about any leaks at Mom's house? She said something about the roof needing repair."

"I haven't seen any leaks," Tommy said. "But I wasn't looking for any, I guess."

"All right. I'll see you tomorrow. Good night, Tommy."

"Good night, Gince," he said. "And thanks again."

Rick was already asleep when Gincy climbed into bed next to him some time later, a magazine open on his chest, his reading glasses still on his nose. Carefully, Gincy removed the glasses and put the magazine on her own nightstand. She wished she could talk to her husband about the conversation with her mother and what she was planning, but that would have to wait until morning.

Gincy leaned back against the pillows. She was nervous about this visit home to Appleville, there was no denying it. And she hoped that Tommy would keep his promise not to tell their mother she was coming. If Ellen Gannon knew that her daughter was planning to visit and why, she might very well refuse to have her; she was famous for having a very wide stubborn streak and a sometimes overly large sense of pride. And even if her mother did agree to a visit, Gincy preferred the advantage of surprise so that she could see what was really going on in the house on Crescent Road.

She glanced at her bedside clock. It was already closing in on eleven. Time to get some sleep. Gincy leaned down and kissed Rick good night, careful not to wake him. Then she turned out the light on her nightstand and tried to mentally prepare herself for whatever tomorrow would bring.

CHAPTER 4

The next morning Gincy packed her overnight bag, iPhone, and laptop and prepared for a trip to Appleville. Although she was reluctant to take unscheduled time off work, she was confident that her excellent assistant could handle things for a few days without her.

Tamsin, on her Christmas break from school, insisted on coming along, and while Gincy appreciated her daughter's offer and had no doubt as to its sincerity, she still thought Tamsin was a little bit nuts. What kind of fifteen-year-old girl, and a social and popular one at that, would choose to spend her precious Christmas vacation with her often cantankerous grandmother rather than with her BFFs, ice-skating, shopping for stuff they didn't need, and going to holiday blockbuster movies?

A really nice fifteen-year-old girl, Gincy thought. A girl with a big heart. A daughter any parent would be proud of.

Rick saw them to the door of the loft.

"Do you have the case for your retainer?" he asked Tamsin.

"Yup," she said. "And I even remembered to pack my phone charger!"

"Let me know if you need me to join you," Rick said to his wife. "You're not the only one with a competent assistant and a well-oiled staff. The office can live without me for a day or two."

"I'll be fine," Gincy said, hoping that would prove to be true. "I can handle my mother."

"I promise to let you know if we need your help, Dad," Tamsin said. "You know how Mom can be around Grandma."

Rick frowned. "I know all too well."

"I'm right here, you two," Gincy protested. "I can hear you. And how *am* I around my mother, anyway?"

"Impatient," Tamsin said.

"Rude," Rick added. "Argumentative. But only sometimes."

He wisely closed the door to the loft, and Gincy's reply was drowned out by the clanging of the jingle bell.

Gincy glanced over at her daughter. Tamsin was wearing earbuds and listening to who knew what ridiculous music. Today's pop music culture, what little Gincy felt compelled to know of it in order to keep an eye on what might be influencing her child, left her feeling slightly queasy. Maybe all fifty-year-olds viewed the popular culture of the younger generations with disdain. But seriously, how could you have any respect for lyrics with rhymes as bad as *lover* and *smother*, *angel* and *fundamental*, *heart* and *die-hard*? The real poets would turn in their graves. And songs about girls allowing their underarm hair to grow? What was the world coming to?

Yikes, Gincy thought. *I've become my mother.* The thought was unsettling for all sorts of reasons, not the least of which was the fact that she had spent a good deal of her adult life purposely distancing herself from what she saw as every negative personality trait her mother displayed, like her fondness for gossip—to be fair, Ellen was never malicious, and sometimes even Gincy, who claimed to hate gossip, found herself listening excitedly to a colleague's whispered stories of scandal—or whatever narrow-minded opinion her mother held, like her complete distrust of the Internet and microwaves and any gadget more complicated than the toaster. Though again, to be fair, there were moments when Gincy herself was convinced that the devil was behind the ridiculously unstable WiFi service in her home.

And she had distanced herself from her mother physically, too. Maybe she should have gone home at least once after her father's funeral but she hadn't been invited and there had been no distress calls until Tommy's call the day before, and without the benefit of getting to spend time with her father, the incentive just wasn't there.

Gincy realized that she had sighed aloud. She was still processing the fact that Ed Gannon would pay no more visits to his family in Boston. There would be no more walks through the Public Gardens and no more meals at the Daily Catch, her father's favorite restaurant in the North End. And there would no more visits to old cemeteries in the city and as far away as Lexington and Concord. Gincy and her father loved old cemeteries. Tamsin thought her mother and grandfather were ghoulish.

"Everyone there is dead," she would say. "It's depressing."

To which her grandfather would reply, "Your mother and I aren't dead. And we go there to acknowledge that those people were once alive. I'm sure it makes them feel good."

Tamsin had never been convinced.

"It's a break from Mom," Gincy would tell Rick every time her father visited, which was usually three or four times a year—not that she needed to apologize for his presence or to ask her husband's permission for him to be there. "The poor guy needs a rest from her constant criticizing, and he badly needs a decent meal. You've had my mother's three bean casserole."

To which Rick would grimace and reply, "And barely survived to tell the tale."

It was interesting, Gincy thought, that not once in all those years had her father ever engaged in conversation about Tommy. All he would say when she asked what her brother was up to was, "Well, you know how he is," or "Well, you know Tommy." Ed Gannon believed that if you didn't have something nice to say about someone, you should say nothing at all. Not for the first time, Gincy wondered why so often she couldn't seem to follow that simple rule of behavior.

Above all, be kind. If those exact words weren't in the Bible as one of the Commandments, Gincy thought, they should be. Do unto others what you would have them do unto you, and above all, be kind.

Suddenly, the car in the left lane sped up and darted in front of Gincy's Volvo. With some effort she refrained from shouting a particularly nasty word. Though plugged in to her music, Tamsin still might be able to hear her mother, and Gincy tried—she really did—to set a good example. She shot another glance at her daughter and thought it likely that Tamsin hadn't even noticed that they had been cut off by a lunatic in a Mazda. She was mouthing the no doubt silly lyrics of whatever song she was listening to, probably something to do with hookups and breakups, oblivious to the world around her.

Tamsin would be getting her driver's permit before long, and Tamsin behind the wheel of a car was not a thought to inspire confidence in her mother. She was a smart kid, just not always the most focused. Rick didn't share his wife's fears to anywhere near the same extent. "Learning how to drive is a step toward her eventual independence," he would say. "We went through it with Justin. The whole point of raising a child is to give them all the tools they need to live successfully on their own. The whole point is to let them go."

That well might be, Gincy thought, spotting the reckless driver several cars ahead, but Tamsin was only a sophomore. She had no intention of even thinking about letting Tamsin "go" until she was well out of high school. Maybe college.

And there was a thought. To this day Gincy didn't know for sure if her father had graduated from high school. She had assumed he had, but when she was about twelve some family member had hinted that Ed Gannon had not earned a high school diploma. It had mattered once to Gincy, the thought that her father's education had, for whatever reason, been cut short. What great things might he have done if he had completed his schooling? And then, over time, it had ceased to matter. She had never sought out the truth, and she never would. Not having completed the twelfth grade hadn't prevented Ed Gannon from being a good father and a good grandfather.

Justin had certainly taken to him right from the start, and as Rick was admittedly dangerous around power tools, the handy Ed had become for Justin a sort of Mr. Fix It Hero. Justin had learned so much from his grandfather over the years, and not only about woodworking and basic electrical wiring. He had learned the importance of finishing what you started. He had learned how to be generous with his time and attention, a lesson his father had reinforced.

Tamsin, too, had adored her grandfather, and not only because he spoiled her with a new teddy bear for her collection each time he saw her. They had enjoyed reading storybooks together, and going to the movies, and eating hot dogs at Red Sox games. Gincy couldn't remember her father ever holding her hand when she was small, though he certainly might have. But he always held Tamsin's hand when they went out together, even when Tamsin became a teen.

It was a bit surprising to Gincy that her children cared as much as they did for their grandmother, because they saw her far less often than they did their grandfather; not once in all the years of Ed's excursions to Boston had she ever accompanied him. She hadn't even attended her daughter's wedding in Boston, and though that had hurt Gincy badly, more than her pride had let anyone but Rick know, she had eventually allowed a scar to form over that wound. Her father, she remembered, had been embarrassed by his wife's absence—"She really would like to be here," he had told Gincy repeatedly, "but you know how frightened she is of the city," almost pleading for her to understand and accept this explanation as truth. And it was largely for his sake that she had indeed come to accept—if not to understand—her mother's behavior. This attitude of acceptance had helped her when Ellen Gannon later failed to visit her granddaughter when she was born or to see her grandson graduate with honors from college.

Not, of course, that her mother would ever admit to a genuine fear of the city. No, she preferred to explain her absences from important family events as a result of her never having had any use for cities. Those were her words. "I have no use for cities." In fact, she had boasted to Gincy that she had never stepped foot in any place larger than the neighboring town of Crescentville that had a whopping population of ten thousand. Cities were dirty and dangerous and loud and ugly. It was no good pointing out all the benefits of living in an urban center, like access to museums, and the availability of foods of various cultures, and free concerts in the parks, and great shopping opportunities, and the visual interest of different architectural styles. Ellen Gannon was having none of it.

Gincy recalled a particularly memorable exchange she had had with her mother many years in the past. It certainly hadn't qualified as a conversation; there had been no give-and-take of ideas.

Mrs. Gannon: "I don't know how you can live in that place. Murderers around every corner, and who knows what else. Rats on the sidewalk, just walking along like they own the place."

Gincy: "Mom, I've been living in Boston since I was seventeen and I haven't been murdered yet. Or attacked by a strolling rat."

Mrs. Gannon, ominously: "There's always a first time, Virginia."

"Mom," Tamsin said. She had removed her earbuds. "You're making a weird face."

"I'm thinking of the strolling rats again."

"Did Grandma really say that?"

"The strolling part is mine," Gincy admitted with a smile.

"So you really think Uncle Tommy is right, that there's something wrong with Grandma?"

"That's what we're going to find out."

Tamsin sighed. "I can't imagine how sad I'd feel if my husband died. I mean, how many years were they married?"

"About fifty-five years."

"Yikes," Tamsin said. "I can't even imagine *living* that long!"

"You do know that your father is going to be fifty-seven soon, don't you?"

"I know. Ancient!"

Fifty-five years together . . . You often heard of elderly couples dying within months of each other. The surviving husband or wife simply couldn't bear to live without the beloved spouse. But that couldn't be the case here, Gincy thought. Her parents had not had a great marriage. She wasn't even sure her mother had liked her father, let alone loved him. If Ellen Gannon wasn't criticizing her husband about the most minor things—"You brought home the wrong-size grapefruit, Ed. I asked for small grapefruits and these are clearly medium"—she was bossing him around. "Ed, the garage needs to be cleaned immediately, and while you're at it you can get to those weeds that need digging up."

For the life of her Gincy couldn't recall her mother ever doing something really nice for her husband, like the things she did for Rick—bringing home a bouquet of his favorite flowers for no other reason than that they were his favorite, or going with him to a hockey game when his buddy couldn't make it, even though she hated hockey like the plague. It was the little sacrifices that helped make a life lived together worthwhile.

No, Gincy thought, if curmudgeonly Ellen Gannon was dying of a broken heart, then she, Gincy Gannon-Luongo, was the Queen of Sheba. And that, Gincy thought, glancing down at her L.L.Bean boots, wool peacoat, and old chinos, was highly unlikely.

CHAPTER 5

"Welcome to Appleville," Tamsin read aloud. "Incorporated in 1842. Wow. That's a long time ago."

"Not so long compared to lots of other towns in New England."

"Still, it's cool. History, I mean. It must be fun living in a historic town. You'd probably run into a ghost!"

"You live in a historic city," Gincy pointed out. "You can't beat Boston for historic drama. And I'm sure the place is full of ghosts, if such things exist."

And Gincy suddenly recalled another exchange that seemed to have taken place endlessly in the first years she was living in Boston.

Mrs. Gannon: "I'll never understand why you had to turn your back on all this and go off to Boston, of all places."

Gincy: "What did I turn my back on, Mom? Monster car rallies? Rock-throwing contests? Dog fights?"

Mrs. Gannon: "Don't exaggerate, Virginia. There haven't been dog fights in Appleville in ten years."

Okay, maybe her mother had said fifty or even one

hundred years, but the point was the same. Ellen Gannon couldn't understand why her daughter had left Appleville. Gincy Gannon couldn't understand why her mother had stayed.

As if reading Gincy's mind, Tamsin said, "I don't know why you always talk so negatively about your hometown. Really, Mom, Appleville is so pretty. I mean, there's a gazebo on the town green and little white churches with bell towers. There's an old-fashioned ice-cream parlor, which, by the way, I want to go to again. There are chirping birds all over the place, and everybody's got a cute dog. Well, almost everybody. Who's that man who lives around the corner from Grandma, the one with the shaggy dog that barks like crazy at everyone? Anyway, Appleville is, like, out of a story-book or a movie. What's so bad?"

"You didn't have to grow up here," Gincy said grimly.

"Yeah, but just because you didn't like living here, Mom, doesn't mean that everyone else hated it."

Gincy couldn't help but smile. "How did you become such a reasonable person with such an opinionated person for a mother?" she asked.

"Dad."

A few minutes later Gincy turned the car onto Crescent Road, and a moment after that she pulled into the drive-way of Number Nineteen.

The houses on Crescent Road were almost identical, having been built in the early 1940s as a housing develop-ment. Number Nineteen, like its neighbors, was a fairly small, two-story structure. On the ground floor were the kitchen, living room, powder room, and one small bed-room that had been Tommy's until he finally left home. On the second floor were the bedroom once belonging to Gincy, her parents' room—well, now her mother's room—and a full bathroom. In truth, the bathroom was hardly much larger than the powder room; the tub was very short, and as far as Gincy knew her parents had never used it for anything other than bathing their children when they were young.

A small garage housed the lawn mower, the snowblower, and the Gannons' single car, a fifteen-year-old white Suburu. The small front yard was now bare of grass. Two evergreen bushes, one on either side of the door, provided the only ornamentation. The backyard, not much bigger than the front yard, was equally as bare of decoration. Every summer the small gas grill was rolled out onto the square of concrete just outside the sliding glass door off the kitchen. With it came a round, green plastic table and four chairs. There was a maple tree in the far corner of the yard. Mrs. Gannon had never gone in for planting flowers. "Why bother?" she said. "They only die and then you have to start all over again."

"That's Uncle Tommy's truck," Tamsin noted, as Gincy parked next to the old Ford pickup. "I recognize the bumper sticker. *I Brake for Beer.*"

"It's in worse shape than it was back in the summer. It needs a paint job," Gincy said. "And look, the wheel wells are almost entirely eaten out by rust!"

"Maybe he can't afford a paint job, or to fix the rust problem. Can you fix a rust problem? I'll have to ask Justin. He knows all about that sort of thing."

Dad would have gotten Tommy's truck repaired for him, Gincy thought. *With his own hard-earned money.* She wondered how often—if ever—her parents had said no to the adult Tommy. She remembered her father trying to discipline her brother when he was young. He would scold, appeal to reason, even punish Tommy, though never physically, but the discipline never seemed to take. By the time Tommy was in high school, her father had pretty much lost what little good influence he had had over his son. At least, he had stopped trying to change his behavior. When Tommy was suspended for a week in junior year for having locked a cafeteria worker into the industrial freezer for a half an hour, Ed Gannon had simply shaken his head and apologized to the victim, who miraculously had not pressed charges.

Here goes nothing, Gincy thought as she rang the bell on Number Nineteen. Tommy opened the door almost before she had taken her finger off the bell. He gave her a brief smile. Tamsin launched herself into his arms, and he hugged his niece tightly.

Tommy, Gincy noted, looked more haggard than usual. The smell of stale cigarette smoke clung to him, and his complexion was muddy. "I'm really glad you came, Gince," he said quietly when Tamsin had released him. "I was starting to get . . ."

Gincy frowned. *He was starting to get scared of losing his meal ticket*. And then she reprimanded herself. *Above all, be kind*. It was such a simple notion, and yet one of the most difficult moral guidelines to follow. Why?

"Where's Mom?" she asked.

"She's resting."

"You didn't tell her we were coming, did you?"

Tommy shook his head.

Gincy went into the living room. A quick survey told her that nothing at all had changed. There were the same old crocheted doilies on every suitable surface. There was the same drab upholstery and faded area rugs; the Gannons had never gone in for carpets or for bare wood floors. There were the lampshades that had been repaired several times, and not very professionally at that. There was the arrangement of plastic mums, faded from the original dark orange to a muddy brown. The walls were the same off-white they had always been. The framed prints on the walls—scenes of forests and waterfalls and fields dotted with cows—had been hanging there since Gincy was a child. The colors in the prints were "off"; Gincy had always suspected that her mother had cut the images out of an old magazine and put them in frames from the Dollar Store.

All the same as it had ever been. For Gincy, the house had always lacked any sense of color and light, any sense of style and beauty. Well, she thought now, that wasn't a crime. And she had succeeded in creating her own home of color and light and style and beauty, so why should her mother's decorating choices still bother her? They shouldn't. But they did.

"I'll be back in a minute," Gincy told Tommy and Tamsin. And a minute or maybe two was all she needed to determine that the house, at least the first floor, had been let go. It wasn't in a dangerous state, and no one would get ill living at Number Nineteen—and there were no leaking ceilings—but it needed a very good cleaning and some small though fairly important repairs. She tried to recall her impression of the house six months ago, when she had been in Appleville for her father's funeral. But she could remember nothing. She had been too focused on her own pain and the duties she had been compelled to perform as family spokesperson to pay much if any attention to the state of her old family home. Besides, she and Rick and the kids had stayed at a motel on the outskirts of town. She had spent minimal time at Number Nineteen.

And the time before that, what had she seen then? That visit to Crescent Road had been at least eighteen months before her father's passing. She had stayed only one night—opting to bed down in Tommy's old first-floor room in order to allow her parents their privacy on the second floor—but it had felt like the proverbial eternity. She remembered her father waving as she drove off soon after breakfast the next morning. If he had been disappointed she had not stayed longer, he hadn't said.

Gincy returned to the living room. She felt upset, mostly with herself, but also with . . . with the unfairness of life.

"Why didn't you call me earlier?" she demanded of Tommy. "How could you have let things get this bad? I don't think the toilet in the powder room has been cleaned in weeks, and you can hardly see out of the kitchen window. And the dust on some of the furniture is half an inch thick in places."

Tommy put his hands in the air, in the time-honored gesture of innocence and self-defense. "It's not my fault, Gince. Everyone knows you and Mom hate each other. I figured you wouldn't come until things got really bad."

Gincy was stunned. "I don't hate her," she protested. And she doubted that her mother hated her, either. Hate was a terrible emotion. Not even Ellen Gannon could be guilty of hating her own child. "We just don't see eye to eye on most things."

Tommy smiled a bit. He was missing a top tooth. It had been there six months ago. "You two don't see eye to eye on anything," he said.

She couldn't deny that. "All right," she said. "At least you finally did call me."

Tamsin had been silent during the exchange between her mother and uncle. Gincy felt bad that she had been witness to it. At least they hadn't raised their voices. That was progress of a kind.

"Grandma!"

Ellen Gannon had appeared at the entrance to the living room.

Gincy began to take a step forward and then stopped, at

a loss as to how to greet her mother. She couldn't remember the last time they had hugged, let alone kissed. She did remember putting her arm around her mother's shoulders when they were at the cemetery, her father's flower-covered casket sitting beside that awful gaping hole in the ground. But after a moment, her mother had shrugged off her daughter's encircling arm.

While Gincy stood rooted to the spot, Tamsin gently put her arms around her grandmother and kissed her cheek. Ellen absentmindedly patted Tamsin's back. When Tamsin had released her grandmother, Gincy finally walked over to where Ellen stood and put her hand briefly on her shoulder. She was thinner than Gincy had ever seen her, and her complexion was wan, as if she hadn't seen the light of day in weeks.

"Hello, Mom," she said.

For a split second Ellen looked confused, as if she didn't recognize her daughter, and then she said, "Hello, Virginia. I didn't know you were supposed to be here today."

Gincy felt her stomach sink. How in the world, she wondered, looking at this pale and pathetic figure, had she not picked up on something wrong before now? Had her mother been asking for help in some muddled or enigmatic way that she had been unable or unwilling to hear? Certainly the situation in this house couldn't have happened overnight, and it certainly wasn't Tommy's fault that he hadn't called his sister weeks ago. To blame him was simply wrong.

"Tamsin and I thought we'd surprise you," Gincy said, darting a look at her daughter. "For Christmas."

Tamsin slipped her arm through her grandmother's. "I hope we didn't wake you up when we rang the bell," she said.

Ellen shook her head.

"It's nice that Gince is here, right, Mom?" Tommy said, his tone hopeful.

Gincy glanced again at her brother. Tommy was wearing his usual black concert T-shirt, baggy jeans, and a pair of dirty white sneakers. She wondered if he had proper winter clothing. It was chilly even in the house; her parents had always been very careful with what little money they had, and heat was considered a bit of a luxury. But then she dismissed the thought. Tommy's wardrobe was not her responsibility.

What was her responsibility was her mother. Her father would have been upset to see his wife so unkempt. Ellen Gannon had always been impeccably neat about her appearance, but now her cardigan was wrongly buttoned and her shoes were scuffed. Her thinning hair, usually kept tidy in a tight, low bun, was now loosely held with a clip that looked too heavy to stay put.

Gincy abruptly went back to the kitchen. The others silently followed her. She opened the fridge to find a half-empty carton of orange juice, a quarter stick of butter, and a bag of green beans turned brown and mushy. There was no milk, sour or not. Then she checked the pantry cupboards and was further shocked by what she found. This was not good. "There's nothing in here but a few cans of soup and half a box of crackers," she said, closing the last cupboard and turning to her mother. "What have you been eating, Mom?"

Ellen began to fiddle with one of the buttons on her sweater. The button was loose. "I wish you had told me you were coming," she said. "I would have gotten the house ready. I would have . . ."

"Don't worry about the house," Gincy said firmly. She

felt a growing distress, but she knew she had to maintain a facade of calm and orderly control. She took a seat at the kitchen table. The cloth covering was uncomfortably sticky. She retrieved a small spiral notebook from her bag, slung as always across her chest, and the good old-fashioned Number 2 pencil she always carried and began to write out a detailed shopping list, including what she remembered to be her mother's favorite foods, as well as a wide variety of staples, from breakfast cereal to more canned soups, from dried pasta to frozen peas, from fresh bread to fresh fruit and vegetables. She was aware of her mother, brother, and daughter watching her silently. Their watchfulness and expectation made her feel anxious. They had put her in a position of authority—or maybe she was there by default—and at that moment she wasn't at all sure that she was worthy of their trust.

When she was finished writing, she gave the list to her brother.

"Tamsin will go with you to Harriman's," she said. "Get everything on this list."

Gincy took out her wallet and removed her debit card from its slot. She gave the card to Tamsin, who she had long ago entrusted with her PIN.

"No junk food, Tommy," she warned. "And no cigarettes or beer. Take my car. Here are the keys." Trusting Tommy to drive her own car, a Volvo wagon identical to her husband's, was a risk, but it was better that her daughter be in a vehicle that had passed inspection than in a broken-down old truck that might lose a fender along the way.

"Come on, Uncle Tommy," Tamsin said quietly, and the two went off.

For the first time since her father's funeral, Gincy was alone with her mother. She felt almost as if she was in the presence of a stranger.

"Have you eaten anything today, Mom?" she asked.

Ellen cleared her throat. "Cereal. Some cereal."

But Gincy had seen no cereal in the cupboards. And there was no milk in the fridge. "Can I make you something to eat now?" she asked. "I could open a can of soup. Tommy will be back soon with something more substantial."

"No, thank you, Virginia," Ellen said.

"Are you sure?"

Ellen yawned, careful as always to cover her mouth with her hand. "Excuse me," she said.

At least, Gincy thought, her mother hadn't lost track of social proprieties. That was something. But hadn't Tommy said their mother had been resting when she and Tamsin had arrived? Why was she still tired?

"Are you sleeping well at night, Mom?" Gincy asked.

Her mother shrugged. "Not always. Sometimes I . . ." Her voice trailed off.

"Would you like to take another nap," Gincy said. "Just until Tommy and Tamsin come back with the groceries?"

Ellen slowly got up from the table. "Yes," she said. "I think I will lie down for a while."

Gincy watched her mother walk out of the kitchen. She was surprised and worried by her docility. Ellen Gannon had never been in the habit of agreeing to her daughter's suggestions. In fact, it was her habit to vigorously argue against anything Gincy recommended, whether it be that she try a new recipe or that she see a particular movie or that she buy a decent brand of soap that didn't leave the skin stinging. Her mother would endure any hardship for a bargain, even raw, red skin.

Gincy got up from the table. She would bring her bag and Tamsin's upstairs to her old bedroom, get them unpacked, and make up their beds. There would be much to do in the next few days, and she would get none of it done by sitting around brooding.

Besides, there was still the condition of the second floor to assess, and who knew what mayhem she might find there.

CHAPTER 6

Her mother had been asleep—at least, she had been in her room—for almost an hour, and Tommy and Tamsin were still not back from the store. Gincy considered sending Tamsin a text but refrained. She had given them a long shopping list. Tommy hadn't run them into a ditch. They were just filling up a shopping cart with chicken breasts, paper towels, cartons of orange juice, and the cakes and cookies her mother had always been so fond of.

I need to keep my head, she thought. *I'd better call Rick*.

He answered right away. "You're there?"

"Yeah. Safe and sound in spite of a maniac in a Mazda cutting us off."

"And?" he asked. "What's going on?"

Gincy sighed. "This could take longer than I thought. Mom's clearly depressed and she hasn't been eating. You know how my mother loves to eat."

"I do," he said. "Frankly, it always surprises me that she isn't a better cook. But taste doesn't always come with appetite. I cite the infamous three bean casserole."

Gincy peered into the sink. There was a line of grime all

around the basin that looked as if it had been there for some time. "And the house really has been let go," she said. "Tommy was right. There's a terrible smell of must in the upstairs hall. I hope it's just must and not mold. That could be big trouble. Anyway, you know how house proud my mother has always been, though I've never seen that there's all that much here to be proud of."

"Gincy."

"Sorry. Anyway, what exactly am I supposed to be doing here, Rick? I think I set out without any clear intention, without a plan. I have to tell you I feel a bit overwhelmed, and you know that's not something I often feel."

"You're supposed to be fixing what you can fix," he said. "Focusing on the immediate issues, like seeing if you can get her to eat. And try to get her to talk about what she's feeling. Well, that's not going to be easy—she's not exactly an open person—but take it step by step, Gincy."

"If it were Dad who needed me, I'd know what to do. Things were—things were less complicated."

"I know," Rick said soothingly.

"I sent Tommy and Tamsin for groceries," she told him. "They're taking forever."

"I'm sure they're fine. How does Tommy seem?"

"Upset. He's lost a tooth, Rick."

"Oh."

"Rick? Is it my fault?"

"That Tommy lost a tooth?" Rick asked. "I don't think so, Gincy."

"No, I mean, everything that's going on here. Everything seems to be falling apart. Is it my fault?"

"No," Rick said firmly. "It's not your fault. But it looks like it is your responsibility to do what you can to get things back on track for your mother. And possibly for your brother, but I wouldn't worry about him too much at the moment."

Gincy sighed. "Send me good thoughts, okay? I'll check in again tomorrow. And don't forget to water the tree. I don't want the loft burning down."

Rick promised, "I don't want it burning down either, and with me in it" and signed off.

Gincy looked around her mother's kitchen, at the all too familiar curtains on the small window over the sink, faded now from a once bright yellow; at the linoleum flooring, curling up in places; at the fridge that was at least thirty years old. All the boring, unappetizing dinners she had endured in this room, Tommy kicking his chair, her mother chattering on, complaining, questioning her daughter's every move, her father eating his meal without speaking, other than to ask for the salt or pepper. And Gincy? All she had wanted, while Tommy made noise and her mother whined on and her father busily chewed, was to get out and never come back.

She shook her head. She was going to go nuts standing around waiting for her brother and her daughter to get back from Harriman's. First things first. Step by step, like Rick had said. Hunt down the cleaning supplies and make a list of what additional supplies she would need.

Oh, Dad, she thought, peering into the cabinet beneath the sink where the Windex and the dish detergent and the Clorox was kept, *what have I done?* Because in spite of her husband's reassurance, she didn't quite believe that she wasn't at least partly responsible for the sorry state of affairs at Number Nineteen.

CHAPTER 7

Gincy had prepared their dinner, making do with her mother's ancient and battered kitchenware and appliances. When, she asked herself, was the last time the knives had been sharpened? Dull knives could be as much of a hazard as sharp ones. She had looked briefly around the kitchen for a sharpening steel, but had quickly noted that the drawers hadn't been cleaned (several drawers were littered with crumbs) or organized in an age. There was no way she was going to unearth a particular tool without launching a major and time-consuming search.

Why had her father not seen to the knives, she wondered. Why had he not called the repairman when he realized that only one of the burners on the stove was working? There was one answer that came immediately to mind, and it was an unpleasant one. Ed Gannon had been failing in the final year of his life, and Gincy had not known. Certainly he had never said anything to her during his last visits—assuming he had been aware of his diminished abilities—and her mother had given no indication that Ed might not be as capable as he once was. Had Ellen even noticed? Were her own abilities diminished?

The family sat at the table, Ellen in the chair she had occupied at meals for as long as Gincy could remember. Tommy sat in his usual place, too, and Tamsin sat where Gincy had sat until she had left home at the age of seventeen. Gincy found herself in her father's usual place. She felt a bit like a usurper. *Then again*, she thought, *I am now the one in charge, aren't I?*

"This is great, Gince," Tommy said, chewing vigorously.

"Thanks," she said.

Gincy wondered if her brother's cupboards were bare, too. She wondered if Ellen was giving him some sort of allowance. She would have to find out. Tommy couldn't be allowed to bleed their mother dry, intentionally or not.

Unlike her son, who ate like a starving man, Ellen picked at the chicken breast and baked potato and string beans. The conversation, what there was of it, was uninteresting and largely uninformative. Tamsin asked her grandmother if she was ready for Christmas. From the utter lack of holiday decorations in the house, it was clear that Ellen wasn't, but Gincy was grateful to her daughter for trying to engage her grandmother. "It's Christmas already," Ellen stated flatly. "Time flies by."

Tamsin asked her uncle if he had seen the latest big action movie, the one featuring a group of superhero robots from Pluto. He hadn't. "Maybe we could go while I'm here," Tamsin suggested. Tommy nodded and shoveled a large bite of baked potato into his mouth. At least having a missing tooth wasn't interfering with his ability to eat.

Gincy gave her daughter a smile. Tamsin was a good kid. There was little if any doubt in Gincy's mind that her daughter—and her stepson—would be there for their parents in the future, whatever being "there" turned out to mean. And as she glanced around the table, she wondered what a person really owed to her family. Back when she was young, before she met Rick and her life had changed in so many ways for the better, she used to regard family as a cumbersome thing foisted upon you at birth. Whether you liked it or not, there it was, unavoidable at least until you were old enough to get away and not have to rely on them for food, clothing, and shelter. But even when you were out from under the weight of their daily presence, family was still *there*. Emotionally unavoidable. Ever present.

And now, Gincy thought, she was being called upon to come back and provide—literally or proverbially—the food, clothing, and shelter for what was left of her birth family. Responsibility worked both ways, if you chose to accept your part in the family dynamic. You didn't have to, there was no law that could be enforced, and lots of people did turn their back on the messiness and complications of their parents and grandparents for good as well as for bad reasons.

But I can't do that, Gincy thought now, watching her mother listlessly push bits of chicken around her plate, seeing her brother gulping from the bottle of soda he had bought even though soda had not been an item on Gincy's shopping list, and then wiping the back of his hand across his mouth. *I can't turn away. I wish I could, but I can't.*

When dinner was over and Tamsin and Ellen were settled on the living room couch with the television tuned to some antic game show her mother had been addicted to for years, Gincy walked Tommy out to his truck.

While Tommy was still skinny he had developed the middle-aged beer drinker's gut. And his hair, always thin, was now sparse and almost entirely gray. Had it been gray back at their father's funeral in June? Gincy couldn't remember. *We're getting old*, she thought. *Tommy and me.*

And then there came a wave of sadness that shook her almost physically.

"Where's your coat?" she asked, pulling her own coat closer around her. The temperature had dropped significantly when the sun had gone down at four-thirty.

"At home," he said. "I got some oil on it when I was working on my truck and . . ." He shrugged.

"Is Mom able to drive?"

"She can," Tommy said. "I mean, her eyesight is okay, but she mostly doesn't. Except for church, she doesn't really go anywhere, not since Dad died. Well, she says she goes to church most Sundays, but I guess I don't really know if she does. She doesn't ask me to go with her."

That's why her cupboards were bare, Gincy thought. Her mother wasn't leaving the house.

"She seems overly tired," Gincy said. "Do you know if she's sleeping at night?"

Tommy shrugged again. "She hasn't said anything to me."

Gincy rubbed her forehead. Why hadn't her brother talked to someone at the church, asked if there was a parishioner who could look in on their mother? Why wasn't he being proactive for once in his life and asking his mother the important questions about her health? Are you eating, Mom? Are you sleeping?

Then again, she thought, why hadn't she, the responsible child, the one with a career, marriage, and family, why hadn't *she* been home in six months to visit her newly widowed mother?

"What did you and Mom really do for Thanksgiving?" Gincy asked, dreading the answer she knew was coming. "When I called that morning, she told me she was making the usual turkey dinner for the both of you. She didn't, did she?"

"No," Tommy admitted. "I guess she wasn't up to it.

She sent me to the store for a couple of frozen dinners. They're not bad. I eat them a lot."

Gincy and Rick and Tamsin had served up a feast at their loft, surrounded by good friends and an assortment of pampered children and dogs. It had been a wonderful day, with lots of stimulating conversation and genuine laughter. After the obligatory call to Appleville that morning, Gincy hadn't thought of her mother or her brother once.

Now, the thought of them eating frozen meals at the kitchen table with the sticky tablecloth stabbed at Gincy's conscience, as did the fact that her mother, a brutally honest person, had chosen to lie to her; she had chosen to keep from her daughter the truth of her emotional condition, the fact of the overdue electric bill, the fact of the empty cupboards and the dirty house. Ellen Gannon was proud, and that was all right, but pride unchecked could get you into trouble.

"Are you working?" she asked her brother.

Tommy looked embarrassed. Gincy wasn't sure she had ever seen him look embarrassed, not even the time he had been caught peeing against the wall of the high school by the head of the PTA. Well, Gincy hadn't been there at the time, but she was pretty sure Tommy hadn't been embarrassed, not with the way he had laughed about it afterward.

"Not much," he said. "The guy down at the convenience store needs help stocking shelves sometimes. He gives me cash."

Gincy refrained from a sigh. "Do you need money?" she asked. When, she wondered, was the last time her brother had seen a dentist? Too long a time, obviously. But with no health or dental insurance, and with no steady income, how was he supposed to pay for treatment, let alone go to the latest blockbuster action movie or buy a new coat if the old one really was beyond saving?

Tommy shrugged again. "I'm okay," he said.

He's changed since Dad died, Gincy thought. *He's . . . subdued.* Just how much had Tommy relied on their father for a sense of stability? She had never given it a thought before now, Tommy's needing their father's strong and re-assuring presence. As a child and then as a young man, he had routinely ignored or rejected his father's guidance and good advice. She thought back to the funeral at Ellen's church, how Tommy had sat hunched next to their mother in the front pew, his old, ill-fitting suit jacket hanging off his thin shoulders, his face a mask of pain. *Damn it*, she thought. If she could have managed a kick to her own backside, she would have done it.

"Look, Tommy," she said, "before I go back to Boston, you and I will make some arrangement about Mom. You'll have to shop for her and see that she eats properly. And you might have to hire a local woman to help her clean the house if she can't do it on her own. I'll give you the money for that. Can I trust you with that job, to keep an eye on Mom? Because I can't stay here forever."

Tommy answered stoutly and, Gincy thought, a bit de-fensively, "Yeah, you can trust me," he said. "I would never do anything to hurt Mom."

Gincy nodded. "Did this heap of steel pass inspection?" she asked.

Tommy laid a hand on the door of his truck. "Don't worry about me, Gince." He shivered. "Just take care of Mom."

Easier said than done, Gincy thought. "You're freezing. You should get home."

"Yeah." Tommy turned and climbed into his truck.

"Drive safe," Gincy said. She didn't wait to see her brother pull away but went back inside Number Nineteen to the sound of the truck's engine painfully spluttering to life.

There was no sign of her mother. She had probably gone upstairs to her room again. The room she had once shared with her husband. Tamsin was in the living room, reading a book she had been assigned to report on during the Christmas break. It was a biography of Angelina Jolie. What ever happened to assigning kids biographies of the greats, like Abigail and John Adams, Einstein, Mozart, even Fred Astaire or Ginger Rogers? When Gincy had asked this of Tamsin, Tamsin had said, "Mom, just because they're all dead doesn't make them better than someone who's still alive." Well, Gincy hadn't been able to argue with that.

Now she went into her mother's kitchen to make a cup of tea. A box of decent tea was one of the items she had asked Tommy and Tamsin to bring back from the grocery store. Her mother had always used an obscure, ridiculously cheap brand of tea bag that routinely leaked crushed leaves into the cup. Was it really worth choking on the sharp, little bits of dried leaves in order to save a few cents? Mrs. Gannon might think so, but her daughter did not.

When the tea was ready, Gincy sat at the table. She had vigorously cleaned the cloth both before and after dinner, but it still felt sticky. It should be thrown out and replaced. Gincy added this chore to the growing list she was compiling in her spiral notebook, a list that included finding out the details of Tommy's financial dealings with her mother.

The thing was, she truly believed that Tommy wouldn't intentionally hurt their mother, not at this point in his life, though God knew he had caused her enough heartache in the past. But he might be seduced by one of his buddies, assuming they were still around and hadn't come to unhappy ends, into spending the money she sent him for a cleaning person on alcohol or lottery tickets or cigarettes. Maybe, Gincy thought, remembering her brother's hunched shoulders, the look of embarrassment on his face, maybe it would be better to send a check directly to her mother. But even if her mother accepted the money, and with her pride there was no guarantee that she would, acceptance wouldn't guarantee that she would spend it on groceries or domestic help and not give it away to her son. And there was always the chance that she might forget to cash the check, like she had forgotten to pay the electric bill. A gift card to Harriman's might be the way to go, *if* her mother could be persuaded to leave the house. And as for a cleaning person, Gincy might have to pay her directly, but who would check to be sure she was doing a proper job?

Gincy yawned a yawn that seemed to go on forever. In spite of the dose of caffeine she had just ingested, she suddenly felt exhausted and, as she had told her husband earlier, more than a little overwhelmed. It was time to call an end to this interminable and disturbing day.

CHAPTER 8

Tamsin had already made herself comfortable on the blow-up mattress they had brought with them from Boston. Tamsin was one of those people who could curl up in the most uncomfortable, hard plastic chair or the most saggy, unforgiving couch and be asleep within minutes.

"Hi, Mom," she said.

"Hey." Gincy dropped down onto the narrow bed on which she had slept for most of the first seventeen years of her life. And yes, the bed—along with the dresser with a few missing knobs and the small desk with matching chair—was still here. It always had been, in spite of what she had told her good friends Clare and Danielle all those years ago—that her mother had cleared out the room the moment her daughter had left for college, dumped all of her possessions in the basement where they were left to deteriorate, and installed her sewing machine and other personal belongings in their place.

Why had she lied? Who knew? She had enjoyed being perverse. She had needed to exaggerate the unpleasantness of her home life for some odd, childish reason she no longer wanted to identify. Gincy sighed and tossed her socks into the corner where she had spent her childhood tossing dirty clothes. Well, the sewing machine *was* now here in the room; that much was true. Though if the thick layer of dust covering it was any indication, it hadn't been used in some time.

"Mom?" Tamsin said from under her favorite fleece blanket. It was bright pink. She had brought one of her favorite teddy bears with her, too. This one was the color of caramel and named, appropriately enough, Theodore.

"Yes, Tamsin."

"Did you really see the Rolling Stones?"

"Yeah," she said. "What made you ask that?"

"I found a ticket stub in the drawer of the desk."

"I must have left it there on one of my quick visits home during college. What else did you find while you were snooping?"

"Not much. Nothing interesting, anyway."

Gincy laughed. "Thanks."

"Uncle Tommy didn't have a coat," Tamsin said. "Who doesn't wear a coat in December? Unless you live in Florida or something."

Gincy lay back on the mattress. It was hard and flat. It must never have been replaced after she had moved out. The sheets she had found balled up in the hall closet were familiar, too. The fitted sheet had a tear. "He said it was dirty."

"Oh. But isn't it better to wear a dirty coat than no coat at all?"

"One would think."

"Mom, why is Uncle Tommy the way he is? Was he always so . . ."

"So much of a loser?" Gincy said.

"I don't like using that word about family," Tamsin

replied stoutly. "I was going to say, was he always so lost. I mean, at Grandpa's funeral he looked pretty awful, seriously upset, but now it's like, I don't know, now it's like he's a ghost. Do you know what I mean? It's like part of him isn't here anymore."

"I do know what you mean," Gincy said. "And I'm sorry I used the word loser. What I should have said was that, yes, Tommy was always unsuccessful. He was a poor student. Frankly, I think he might have a learning disability, but as far as I know it was never identified and certainly not addressed. And he never took to sports. He never had much of an interest in anything, really. He never had a hobby, and he never joined a club at school. After a while he was too busy drinking and smoking dope to get involved."

Tamsin sighed. "That's so sad."

Yes, Gincy thought. It was sad. She felt an unfamiliar stab of pity for her brother. The fact was she used to think that Tommy was fairly bright and just lazy and self-concerned, and she had despised him for it. But over time she had come to realize—if slowly and with resistance— that Tommy wasn't bright at all and that laziness and self-interest had nothing to do with his inability to live a productive adult life. Not much, anyway. At least the mean streak he had exhibited early on seemed to have run itself out. And as far as Gincy knew, he hadn't been arrested since his early twenties. That didn't necessarily mean he wasn't committing crimes punishable by law; it might only mean that he was smarter now about not getting caught. Whatever the case, neither she nor her mother was being asked for bail money, and that was something for which to be grateful.

"I know I've got a nasty, suspicious mind," she said then, "but I can't help but wonder if Grandma's depressed mood is really just a bid for attention. She does have a flair for the dramatic, and she can be passive-aggressive, believe me."

Tamsin shook her head. "No way. You know how she loves to eat. Do you really think she'd starve herself just to get our attention? And you know how fanatical she's always been about cleaning. Do you really think she'd stop dusting and vacuuming just so we'd notice? Mom, this is not about you or me or anyone else. It's about Grandma being really, genuinely sad. It's about her missing Grandpa."

"I know," Gincy said. "You're right. Like I said, I can have a nasty, suspicious mind."

"Mom. Don't exaggerate."

I just wish it weren't happening this way, Gincy thought, staring up at the ceiling. It was peeling in spots, she noted. It should be repaired and painted.

But the ceiling—as long as it wasn't leaking—wasn't a priority at the moment. Her mother—and yes, her brother, too—were the priorities. Seeing her mother depressed was a challenge against her long-held belief that Ellen Gannon was basically heartless and untouched by stronger emotions. It made her uncomfortable, this challenge. It made her feel deeply unsure. If she had been so wrong about her mother—and about her brother—what else had she misread or misinterpreted? Who else had she ignored or unintentionally hurt?

Gincy sighed. Rick was wonderfully wise when it came to emotional matters, but at that moment she wished she could ask her father for advice about how to handle her mother and brother going forward. She wished she could ask him for the truth about his relationship with her mother. For the truth about Tommy.

She wished she could ask him for the truth about herself and why she felt that her mother seemed not to like her all that much.

"Good night, Mom," Tamsin said, with a yawn.

"Good night, Tamsin."

Within moments Tamsin was sleeping the sleep of the just, Theodore tucked under her arm.

But it was a long time before Gincy could find any rest.

CHAPTER 9

"Good morning, Virginia. Good morning, Tamsin." Gincy turned from the stove to see her mother settling herself at the table. Her appearance was noticeably neater than it had been the day before, and her hair looked freshly washed. Gincy felt warily hopeful. Maybe, she thought, her mother's condition wasn't as bad as it had first appeared. Everyone had an "off" day every now and then.

"Did you sleep all right, Mom?" she asked, putting a plate of scrambled eggs and bacon on the table in front of her mother.

Ellen sighed. "As well as can be expected. Virginia, you snore. I could hear you right through the wall."

"She's like a walrus!" Tamsin said. "I mean, if they snored. They probably do. Do all animals snore? I wonder if turtles snore."

Ellen picked up her fork and poked at her eggs. "These are too runny," she said. "And the bacon is too crispy. I can't eat any of this."

Well, Gincy thought, this combative, critical woman was certainly more recognizable as her mother than the passive, spiritless woman who had greeted them yesterday. Combative and critical Gincy could handle.

"Why don't you have a piece of cinnamon toast, Grandma," Tamsin suggested. "Mom made a whole bunch."

"Cinnamon makes me cough. I'm fine with just coffee."

We're playing the martyr now, are we? Gincy thought, crunching loudly into her own cinnamon toast. That, too, she could handle.

"I could make some regular toast," Tamsin offered.

But Ellen declined. "Coffee will be enough."

"You have to eat something, Mom," Gincy said firmly. "You've lost a lot of weight. You could be malnourished. I think you should see your doctor."

"Why?" Ellen demanded. "So he can pump me full of drugs so you can bring in your delinquent friends to do despicable things to me?"

Tamsin choked on her orange juice. "Sorry," she mumbled from behind her napkin.

"My God, Mom!" Gincy cried. "What are you talking about?"

But Ellen said no more.

Above all, be kind, Gincy told herself. Her mother needed help, and like it or not as the older, responsible child she was the one who had to get her mother back on her feet, even if that meant listening to crazy accusations of abuse while she was at it.

"Why are you here, anyway?" Ellen demanded, putting her coffee cup down heavily on the table. "Who told you to come?"

Gincy hesitated. She didn't want to rat out her brother. He had done the right thing in calling her, and she didn't want him to be taken to task for it. Only days ago she wouldn't have cared. But now . . . Well, now, strangely enough, she did.

"No one told me to come," she said. "It's the Christmas season. Like I told you yesterday, Tamsin and I just thought we'd pay you a visit."

"A surprise visit. You know I hate surprises."

Yesterday her mother had seemed flustered by their presence; this morning she was clearly annoyed. Well, Gincy thought, annoyance was an improvement over confusion, just as criticism was an improvement over passivity.

"The visit was my idea, Grandma," Tamsin said quickly. "I just thought it would be fun."

Ellen bestowed a smile on her granddaughter. "Who's taking care of your father while your mother is here?" she asked. "Who's seeing to his meals?"

"Dad's taking care of himself, Grandma. He's actually a better cook than Mom."

"Thanks," Gincy muttered.

Ellen frowned and turned to her daughter. "Now that you *are* here, what am I supposed to do with you?"

"Nothing. You don't have to entertain us, Mom. We don't want to be any trouble. In fact, for starters, how about I get down to some cleaning."

"Are you saying I keep a dirty house?"

Tamsin shot her mother a warning look. "Of course not, Grandma. But it is a pretty big place and you're all alone. We just want to help out a bit."

Gincy resisted a frown. She felt badly that Tamsin was in the position of mediator. It wasn't right that the child among them should be burdened with the job of making peace. Maybe, she thought, she shouldn't have let Tamsin come along. She could always call Rick and ask him to come and take her back home. . . .

"I'm so glad to see you, Tamsin," Ellen said, reaching

for Tamsin's hand. "My only granddaughter. Your mother should let me see you more often."

Gincy clenched her fists on her lap. *Okay*, she thought. *Tamsin stays, at least for the moment.*

"I hope your mother doesn't allow you to date," Ellen went on. "You're too young to have anything to do with boys, though I never could control your mother when she was your age."

Gincy's cup rattled against her teeth. Tamsin's eyes widened. "Uh," she said, "I'm allowed to date if I want to, Grandma, but I don't want to."

Ellen suddenly released her granddaughter's hand and turned to Gincy. "Your father used to mow the lawn," she said. "Now who's going to do it?"

"How about Tommy?" Gincy suggested.

Ellen frowned. "Tommy has so much to do, Virginia. I hate to ask him."

Above all, be kind. "What does he have to do?" Gincy asked. "He told me he works only part time at the convenience store. Mom, I'm sure he'd be happy to help out if you just asked him."

And her mother would *have* to ask him, Gincy thought, because it would never occur to Tommy to offer help. He was not used to being relied upon. He might even feel that his offer of help would be automatically rejected. It was an unsettling thought. Everyone needed to be needed. Everyone needed a place in the chain of social responsibility. No man or woman was an island. It was something Ed Gannon often said.

"Mom's right," Tamsin said. "I'm sure Uncle Tommy would be happy to help. But how about we talk to him about the lawn when spring comes, okay? There's no use worrying about mowing the grass in December."

But who's going to shovel the snow? Gincy wondered.

Tommy had never been strong, and she had no idea when he had last been to a doctor. She wasn't at all sure he had the strength—or the heart health—to lift their father's old shovel or to push the old snowblower. She would have to arrange something before she went back to Boston, maybe find a local kid willing to do the job for not too much money. Luckily, it had been an oddly mild winter so far. What little snow had fallen had simply melted away.

"And the roof," Ellen said now. "What am I going to do about the roof? Your father said something about the roof, but I can't remember what."

Tamsin looked helplessly at her mother. Gincy got up from the table. "Don't worry about the roof, Mom," she said. "I'll take care of it. Now, how about I make you a bowl of oatmeal?"

Ellen sighed. She seemed suddenly drained of the cantankerous energy she had possessed only a moment ago. "All right, Virginia," she said. "Whatever you say."

CHAPTER 10

Ellen ate most of the oatmeal Gincy had prepared for her, complaining only that it was too hot.

"Wait a few minutes before taking a spoonful," Gincy had advised.

"Or blow on it, Grandma," Tamsin had suggested. "That will work."

Around midmorning, Gincy heard a small thud from the direction of the front hall. "The mail comes early here, I see," she said. "I'll get it."

She returned to the kitchen a moment later with a sheaf of coupons from a pharmacy chain, a postcard advertising a local real estate agency, and what were obviously a few Christmas cards. Gincy scanned the envelopes. They were addressed to Ellen Gannon. To Mrs. E. Gannon. To Mrs. Edward Gannon. None were addressed to Mr. and Mrs. Gannon, for which Gincy was grateful. She had tried to be thorough when sending out word of her father's death to the family in other areas of the state, as well as to the Appleville community. But you never knew what obscure Gannon relation might decide to pop up after years off the grid, assuming that Cousin Eddie was alive and well and tactlessly, if innocently, reminding his wife that he was not.

Traditionally, Ellen displayed the Christmas cards on the narrow mantle over the gas fireplace in the living room. But this year, Gincy had noted, the mantle was bare. What holiday cards her mother had already received sat in a messy pile on a small end table next to the couch.

"Why don't you open these, Mom," Gincy suggested now, holding out the small stack of cards just arrived.

Ellen stared at them. "Oh," she said. "I thought I already had."

"Not these. These are new. Here, this one's from Aunt Lydia."

Ellen took the envelope Gincy handed her and peered at it through her reading glasses. "Is she still alive? I thought she would be dead by now."

"Why?" Tamsin asked. "Has she been sick?"

Ellen didn't answer.

"If Aunt Lydia had died," Gincy said, "her daughter would have told you."

Ellen frowned. "Not all daughters are good and dutiful to their mothers."

With some effort, Gincy kept her mouth clamped shut. The goal was to get through this visit without doing something she would regret. Like strangling her mother.

"Have you sent out your Christmas cards yet, Mom?" she asked.

Ellen shook her head. "I bought a few boxes of cards at the Dollar Store right after Christmas last year," she said, "but I guess I haven't gotten around to sending them out. They're in that cupboard over the fridge."

This was indeed unusual, Gincy thought, remembering now the missing Thanksgiving card. Her mother always had her Christmas cards out by early December. She liked to be the first among her friends and family to announce the start of the holiday season. In addition to being proud and stubborn, Ellen Gannon—like her daughter—was competitive.

"We could help you write them out," Gincy said, retrieving the boxes. She doubted she had seen less attractive or flimsier cards in her lifetime. "Do you have any stamps?"

Ellen shrugged. "There might be a few in the drawer to the right of the sink. I haven't been to the post office in a while."

Gincy checked the drawer. "Ten stamps," she said. "I'll get more today."

"Come on, Grandma," Tamsin said. "I'll help you address the envelopes, okay?"

Without comment, Ellen fetched her ancient address book from another drawer and brought it to the table.

"You've had that book since I was a kid," Gincy said. "Isn't it time you got a new one? Look at it. It's so crammed with old addresses and crossed-out phone numbers, you can hardly find the current addresses. And the binding is broken."

"It serves me just fine," Ellen said. "There's no need to spend money on a new address book."

"I could buy you a new one today. It could be an early Christmas present."

"No, thank you, Virginia," Ellen said, more firmly now. Then she turned to Tamsin. "You know," she said, "your mother and father never had a real wedding here in Appleville."

Gincy opened her mouth to protest this oft-repeated complaint, but once again she got the better of herself. *Above all, be kind*, she thought. *Think of Dad before you open your mouth.*

"I'll be back soon," she announced. "I have a few errands to run."

Ellen turned a page in her address book and didn't respond. Gincy leaned down to whisper to her daughter. "Will you make your grandmother lunch if I'm not back by twelve-thirty or so?" she asked.

"Sure, Mom," Tamsin whispered back.

"And call me if you need anything. I'll try to be quick."

"Don't worry, Mom. And Mom?"

"Yeah?" Gincy said.

"It'll all be okay."

Gincy smiled at her daughter, but she wasn't at all sure she believed that it would.

Chapter 11

Appleville Park was a charming spot in the spring, summer, and fall. Beds of seasonal flowers were kept well watered, and the wide sweep of immaculate lawn was perfectly even like the proverbial carpet. A large stone birdbath attracted a variety of small birds, eager for a drink and a bath. The gentle splashing sound of the little fountain at the center of the birdbath was one of the few entirely pleasant memories Gincy held of Appleville. As soon as she was old enough to get about on her own—she remembered her first bike, a hand-me-down from a male cousin—she would come to the park just to listen to the music of the fountain.

But at this time of year the fountain was silent, the flowers were gone, and the birds were nowhere to be found. Appleville Park presented a bleak and barren aspect typical of winter in New England, grim and gloomy without a blanket of pristine white snow. If you were happy, the monotone gray landscape could make you weep. If you were unhappy, it could make you head right back home with a vow not to leave the house again until the first forsythia had flowered. There were good reasons so many New

Englanders flew off to warm climes for as long a part of the winter as they could afford.

And not only New Englanders, Gincy thought. Danielle Leers Lieberman, one of her two closest friends, made a habit of traveling south each winter, even if it was only for a long weekend. She and her husband, Barry, along with their three daughters, who ranged in age from ten to seventeen, lived in New York, a state far enough north that it experienced its own notably brutal periods of snow, ice, and biting winds.

Then again, not everyone who lived in one of the northern states wanted an escape from below-freezing temperatures. Clare Wellman Livingston, the other of Gincy's closest friends, lived in Maine with her husband, Eason, also a teacher, and their eight-year-old son named Sam. When they weren't skiing or snowboarding or ice-skating, they were camping—yes, even in January—and ice-fishing, something Gincy could never imagine doing.

Danielle. Clare. Gincy. An unlikely trio at first, their friendship had only grown stronger over the years since they had first met while renting a house together on Martha's Vineyard one summer. The women had kept in close touch over the years in spite of their demanding lives, what with spouses and children and careers, and now, in Gincy's case, with the death of a parent. Clare and Danielle had always known that the relationship between Gincy and her mother was toxic—they had been insanely supportive and sympathetic when Ellen was a no-show at Gincy's wedding, even pretending not to notice the tears Gincy was struggling to hold back—and when Ed Gannon died, they had openly wondered what would become of that relationship now that he was no longer around as the only real cement between the women. Gincy had flippantly told her friends that she was planning to wash her hands of the old curmudgeon, but neither Clare nor Danielle had believed her.

"You can be a lot of bluster," Danielle had told her, "but at heart you're a good person. And you'll just have to deal with that."

Clare had said, "Gincy, you always do the right thing. Why pretend otherwise?"

Both women had offered to come to Ed's funeral, but Gincy had refused their kindness. Neither had ever met Ellen Gannon, or Tommy, for that matter, and Gincy had been very keen to keep the situation exactly the way it was. In the end, Clare and Daniel had sent flowers to the funeral home and a personal note of condolence to Mrs. Gannon. Gincy remembered quite clearly her mother showing her the notes and saying, "You've been remiss, Virginia. I don't know why I've never met these friends of yours." What had she replied? She couldn't recall.

Gincy dug in her pocket for her phone and, after taking off her glove, pressed the button that would connect her with Danielle.

"Is matricide ever okay?" she asked without bothering to say hello, shoving her hand back into the glove.

"No!" Danielle replied loudly. "What's going on? Where are you?"

Gincy told her friend that she had arrived in Appleville yesterday afternoon.

"Tommy called me," she said. "He thought something strange was going on with Mom. He was right. I think she's depressed."

"And you haven't even been there twenty-four hours and you're already considering murdering a depressed old woman?"

"Well, she had to complain for like the thousandth time that Rick and I didn't have a real wedding. It *was* a real wedding! Legally binding, legally witnessed. I even wore a dress. Me! And she would have known that firsthand if she had gotten past her crazy hatred of Boston and come with my father. Not that it bothered me, her not being there. I mean, she's only my mother, for Pete's sake. Why should she have made the effort to witness her only daughter tie the knot?"

"I thought you got past that all."

"I did. But sometimes . . ." Gincy found that she couldn't go on.

"Look, Gincy, I know you had a real wedding," Danielle said patiently. "I was there. So was Clare. We were your witnesses. And Justin carried the ring, just in case you've forgotten that, too."

"Of course I haven't forgotten," Gincy said, rolling her eyes to the featureless landscape. "It just drives me crazy that Mom thinks a wedding is not 'real' if it's not a traditional service at the local church with a reception in the basement afterward. It's bad enough we had to endure the party back here a few months later. Three different kinds of ambrosia salad, gloppy casseroles made with mystery meat, and a few buckets of KFC for good measure. And then she complained that I don't let her see Tamsin more often. Well, if she just got on a bus once in while, she could see her all she wanted!"

"Gincy." Danielle's tone was firm and commanding. "Take a deep breath and listen to me. First, for all we know your mother really does have an anxiety disorder that makes her genuinely fearful of noise and crowds and tall buildings. Phobias like that are real, and they can be bad. Second, you know your mother's not suddenly going to stop complaining about not having had the opportunity to be Mother of the Bride in a fancy chiffon dress so she could lord it over her Appleville friends with single daughters. And from what you've told me over the years, she's not the kind of woman to stop bringing up a painful topic just because you ask her to. So, what's left? If you can't change something, accept it."

Gincy laughed grimly. "Adapt and survive. Easier said than done. But you're probably right. Tamsin is with me, by the way. She wanted to come. The kid's a saint."

"Rick's genes, obviously. Look, if your mother is still grieving, and I don't see why she wouldn't be, now is not the time to antagonize her, so remember to be nice."

"I know, I know." Gincy sighed. "I have to admit that seeing her yesterday for the first time since Dad died, well, it was a shock. She's lost a lot of weight, she seemed so confused, and the house is in bad shape. It scared me, Danielle. I felt so responsible, like I'd been ignoring her since my father died, and I have been. And yet, this morning Mom seemed so much more like her old self that she managed to infuriate me all over again!"

"That doesn't mean she's not in trouble," Danielle said. "That doesn't mean she doesn't need your help."

"I know. Let's change the subject. Tell me about the girls."

"I just posted a whole bunch of new photos on Facebook," Danielle said. "You know Michelle turned seventeen last week—thanks for the card and the check, by the way—and we hosted an enormous party at the house. That girl is so popular. I mean, *everyone* likes her, from the jocks to the hipsters to the nerds, or whatever they're called these days. It was insanely fun. And Mykaela just got the first round of braces on her teeth, and she says they hurt terribly. It's the pressure that does it. She is *not* happy but she's a trooper, she'll get through it. She's amazingly resilient."

"And Marissa?" Gincy asked. "How is she?"

"Marissa is her father's daughter all around," Danielle said. "Straight As almost without trying. She's only a freshman but she's already talking about what college she wants to go to, and let me tell you, none of them are party schools!"

"You've become your mother," Gincy said, smiling. "She always thought you and your brother were absolutely perfect. Your father thought so, too."

Danielle laughed. "I am perfect! But you're right. I spoil my children, not to the point where they're insufferable—all my girls are well-behaved you know, and they earn their allowances, believe me, and they treat their grandparents with respect—but I do like them to be aware of their inherent value."

"I think that Rick and I have done a pretty decent job instilling in Justin and Tamsin a belief in their inherent value," Gincy said. "At least, I hope we have. As for my mother, I don't think she's ever been familiar with the concept. Certainly not where Tommy and I were concerned."

"A person can offer only what's in her possession to give, Gincy. Your mother gave you what she had to give, no more and I'm sure no less. Let it go. There's no point obsessing over what did or didn't happen in the past."

"You're right, Danielle," Gincy said after a moment. "And I do promise to try to stop fighting what's gone by, if only for the sake of my own sanity."

"Good," Danielle said firmly.

"Look, I've got to get going. I'm freezing my butt off sitting out here on a bench in the cold."

"Why aren't you in your car with the heater turned on full blast?" Danielle asked.

"I'm a glutton for punishment and self-deprivation, you know that."

Danielle sighed, and Gincy imagined her shaking her

head. "You haven't learned anything from me in all these years, have you? When was the last time you treated yourself to a massage?"

"Never. Bye."

"Good-bye, Gincy."

When life gives you lemons, Gincy thought, getting stiffly up from the bench, *make lemonade.* It was one of Ed Gannon's favorite clichés. Make something good out of something bad. It wasn't much different from Danielle's advice. If you can't change something, accept it. Let it go.

Gincy got into her car and turned the heat up full blast. She was glad she had called Danielle, and she was grateful for such a good friend. When she first met Danielle, she had thought she was an airhead, one of those women totally focused on her looks and oblivious to the really important things in life. Well, Danielle had proved to be more than just what she appeared. All three of them had, actually—Danielle, Clare, and Gincy.

All during that amazing, transformative summer, now twenty years in the past.

CHAPTER 12

Gincy continued on into the heart of town. After a quick stop at the post office for stamps—she chose stamps featuring Santa Claus; she figured her mother would have no objection to Santa Claus—she headed on to the grocery store. Tommy had worked as a checkout person at Harriman's in his midtwenties. He had somehow managed to keep the job for almost three years before being fired, for what misbehavior Gincy never knew. It was the longest time he had ever held a job.

Today's shopping list was composed solely of cleaning products. Gincy was determined to wash every bit of fabric in the house, from couch coverings to curtains, including the better pieces of her father's clothing, still, according to Tommy, in the bedroom closet and old dresser; if the clothes were to be given away, as Ellen had said at the funeral that she wanted them to be, they should be cleaned first. Maybe that would eliminate some of the musty smell that had worried Tommy.

It's the perfect Christmas getaway, Gincy thought, climbing out of her car in the parking lot and stepping into a half-frozen puddle of water in the process. *House cleaning and laundry in Appleville, New Hampshire!*

It had been years since she had last been in Harriman's, but nothing much had changed and she had no trouble locating the cleaning supplies, just where they always had been. And it was there, by the mops and sponges and stain removers, that she spotted her old friend Chrissy Smith. They had gone to grammar school and high school together and just after graduation, Chrissy had married her longtime sweetheart. Over the years Gincy's mother had given her updates on her former classmate, but truthfully Gincy had never paid much attention. She did remember that Chrissy had had her first child before she was twenty. She could be a grandmother by now, and probably was.

It was Chrissy who spoke first. "Gincy!" she cried.

Gincy smiled. She had last seen Chrissy at Ed Gannon's funeral, but they hadn't really gotten to speak. Now Gincy noted that life in Appleville seemed to have agreed with her old friend. Chrissy was attractively plump—she had been a scrawny youngster, like Gincy—and nicely dressed. Around her neck she wore a long chain with a gold locket in the shape of a heart. It looked like an antique, and a good quality one at that.

"I'm sorry I didn't get to say more to you at the funeral back in June," Chrissy said now. "We were all so sorry when we heard the news that your father had died. Me, Marty, and the rest of the family."

Gincy felt tears threatening. She had never been a weeper and her reaction to Chrissy's sympathy, expressed six months after the fact of her father's passing, surprised her. "Thank you," she said.

"Marty always said it was too bad when Ed Gannon re-tired from the hardware store. He said Ed was the only one who really knew what he was doing."

"Thanks," Gincy said again. "He really loved that job."

"So, are you back home for Christmas? Your mom must be so happy."

Gincy managed a smile, and Chrissy went on. "I used to love seeing your parents walking down by the pond out along Margery Road. I can see the pond from my house, you know. Not that I was spying on them! But it was so nice to see a couple that'd been married for so long still hold-ing hands. Every Saturday afternoon, around three o'clock, right up until your father passed, rain or shine. It was, well, it was inspirational."

Gincy felt her heart begin to thud in her chest. Her par-ents held hands? The Gannons were an inspirational cou-ple? Who was Chrissy talking about? Not the mother and father she knew! But . . . Gincy thought hard. When was the last time she had really spent any length of time with both parents? More to the point, when had she last had an open mind about their relationship?

At a loss for a reply, Gincy asked after Chrissy's own parents, and after a few further niceties were exchanged, Chrissy said she had to dash. "There's always so much to do at the last minute," she said. "I've still got a few Christ-mas presents to buy!"

Gincy watched her old classmate turn into the next aisle. Though the meeting had been pleasant enough, it had left her feeling somehow disoriented. *I'm an alien here in Appleville*, she thought. That was to be expected. It was understandable. She hadn't lived in Appleville for over thirty years. But she was an alien in her birth family, too, wasn't she. And somehow that didn't seem right, expected, or understandable.

With as much haste as she could, Gincy filled her shopping cart with cleaning products and took them up to the checkout lines. She was eager to get back to Number Nineteen Crescent Road before she ran into another living reminder of the past she had so firmly rejected.

CHAPTER 13

That big stone building on the right. Gincy frowned. Hadn't that once been a bank? Now, according to the sign on the grounds out front, it had been converted to condos and was known as the Appleville Estates. Gincy remembered the interior of the building, at least the ground floor, with its high ceilings and scrolling plasterwork and marble floors. Those apartments must be gorgeous, she thought. And expensive. Was there now real money in Appleville? Had it become a bedroom community for those who had good jobs in the closest big cities? If that was the case, it was news to Gincy. But things changed. They always changed.

Correction, Gincy thought. Not always. There, coming up on the left, was the high school. At least on the outside it was exactly the same as she remembered it—imposing red brick put together with no obvious reference to grace or style. It had always reminded Gincy of a prison. Even the big sign on the lawn looked the same, though it was probably a replica of the one that had been there when Gincy was a student. A lot of years had passed since then. A lot of wear and tear.

Gincy sighed and drove on. *How would my life have been different if I had never gone away to college*, she wondered. *How would it have been different if I had come back to Appleville after graduating from Addison University?* She wondered if her relationship with her mother—and her brother—would be better than it was now if she had never left or if she had returned to the family fold. She wondered if she ever would have grown close to her father in the way that she had if she hadn't first put some distance between them.

She tightened her hands on the wheel. It was silly even to consider the idea of a life lived in Appleville. It never, ever could have happened. She would have to have been a completely different person right from the start. She would have to have been Chrissy Smith. She would have to have been a person who felt content with her lot. And she had been anything but content as a young person, certainly not after the age of thirteen. Contentment had only come with time, with marriage and children, with Rick and Justin and Tamsin and the life they had built in Boston.

When Gincy pulled into her mother's driveway and got out of her car, shopping bags full of laundry detergent, stain remover, and bleach in tow, she noticed the neighbor to the right, Adele Brown, waving to her from her front step.

Suddenly, Gincy remembered how she used to rant on about the town being overrun with Browns. When she was young she used to claim, based on nothing more than a superior, snarky attitude, that actual inbreeding had taken place, but now she suspected the truth was far less dramatic and that there were actually two or more large unrelated families with the surname Brown occupying Appleville. *What a jerk I used to be*, she thought. *And for what? What did it get me? The good things I've achieved in my life have all been due to hard work and to kindness.*

Adele Brown now motioned for Gincy to join her. Gincy put down the shopping bags and began to cross the lawn. "Will you come inside for a moment?" Adele asked when Gincy was close enough to hear.

Gincy followed her into the tiny entrance hall characteristic of all the houses on Crescent Road.

"I won't keep you," Adele said. "I just wanted to apologize for not having called you about your mother."

Gincy felt that sense of alienation again. Alienation and disorientation. "What do you mean?" she asked.

"Well," Adele explained, "of course I noticed that she didn't seem to be eating. I mean, it was obvious. Her clothes started to hang off her. And the few times I stopped by with a pound cake or a streusel—your mother does love my baking, so I thought it would tempt her to eat—I couldn't help but notice that her housekeeping wasn't as, well, as good as it had been. And sometimes she puts the trash out on the wrong day. Pick up is Thursday around here. Those times she puts the trash out on a Tuesday or Wednesday, my husband, you've met Mike, he goes over and takes care of it. He brings the bags back here and we put them out with our trash on the right day. We don't want to embarrass your mother by pointing out her mistakes."

"That's very kind of you," Gincy said. "Thank you."

"No worries. I did ask Ellen once, about a month ago, if she wanted me to call you, but she said no and she was emphatic about it. She said she didn't want to bother you, what with your big, important job in the city. She insisted that she was fine, that nothing was wrong." Adele put her hand briefly on Gincy's arm. "But she isn't fine, is she?" she asked.

Gincy felt her throat tightening again. *Don't cry*, she

commanded herself. She had no choice but to face the truth. She was at least partly responsible for having caused the situation in which her mother found herself, alone, depressed, confused—and assuming that her daughter would not want to be bothered by a lonely old woman. Gincy wondered what the people of Appleville must think of Ellen Gannon's daughter. *And why do I care*, she wondered. But she did care. More than she ever thought that she would.

"It's okay, Adele," she said finally. "You have nothing to apologize for. You've been a good neighbor. Anyway, I'm here now. Hopefully things will be . . . I'll do what I can."

Adele smiled. "You'll let me know if there's anything else Mike and I can do, won't you?"

"I will," Gincy promised. "And thanks again for taking care of the garbage situation."

Gincy left the Browns' house and retrieved the shopping bags from where she had left them by the car. The door to Number Nineteen was unlocked and Gincy went inside. For a moment she stood in the tiny entry hall, shopping bags hanging from her hands. She had always prided herself on being responsible, on having a strong sense of duty, but where her mother was concerned she had been neglectful. There was no way around that startling fact, no matter how strongly her husband argued it.

"Better late than never" is what her father used to say. But was that really true? Sometimes, Gincy thought, it must be too late to help.

She hoped this wasn't one of them.

CHAPTER 14

"Is Tommy coming for dinner?" Tamsin asked.

Gincy, once again battling with her mother's unpredictable appliances, shrugged. "I have no idea. Better set four places, just in case."

When she had finished setting the table, Tamsin joined her mother at the stove. "Mom," she said, voice low. "Grandma was really upset when we were writing out the Christmas cards this morning. She kept signing her name *and* Grandpa's and then getting angry and tearing up the cards. I'm not sure we should have talked her into doing it."

Gincy sighed. "Sensitivity never was my strong point. I didn't even think about that part of the process and how it might upset her. I should have. I was glad that no one had sent a card addressed to the two of them. I knew *that* would upset her. Did she get any cards completed?"

"A few. I put them in the mailbox on the corner. But Mom, even her handwriting is different now. It's shaky."

"That's not uncommon with older people," Gincy pointed out. "Grandpa's handwriting became almost illegible by the time he was seventy."

"But back in the spring, before Grandpa died, her hand-writing was fine. I remember because she sent me a nice card for my birthday."

Before Gincy could respond to this—and what could she say?—her mother joined them.

"Where were you all afternoon?" Ellen asked peremptorily. "You never told me."

"Hello, Mom," Gincy said. "I wasn't gone all afternoon; I was back by one. And I didn't tell you where I'd gone because you were taking a nap when I came in. Anyway, I went to the post office and then I went shopping for more cleaning supplies. I ran into Chrissy Smith at Harriman's. She said again how sorry she was about Dad."

Ellen nodded. "She's always been a nice girl."

"Who is Chrissy Smith?" Tamsin asked.

"Someone I went to grammar school and high school with," Gincy explained. "She was at Grandpa's funeral, but I don't think you met her."

"She's lived in Appleville all her life," Ellen said. "Raised her children here, and now she's a grandmother. It's too bad her son moved away. She never sees those grandkids."

"Why did he move away?" Tamsin asked.

Ellen waved her hand dismissively. "He got some job offer in Chicago, at one of those big universities where they teach all sorts of things and who knows what else."

"He's a professor?" Tamsin asked.

"A doctor of something, yes. It's a real shame."

"But Grandma," Tamsin argued, "that means he's smart and ambitious. Don't you think his parents are proud of him?"

Gincy waited for her mother's reply, but Ellen said nothing.

"Sit down, Mom," Gincy said. "Dinner's almost ready."

Ellen took her seat.

"Where's Tommy?" Tamsin asked, pouring them each a glass of water.

"He's a grown man," Ellen said. "He has his own life. He doesn't need to report in to me."

Gincy brought the meal to the table—sliced steak, mashed potatoes, and carrots—and took her seat. "So he just shows up when he wants to?" she asked.

"Well, there's nothing wrong with that. I am his mother. He's welcome here."

But I'm not welcome because I'm the one who moved away and keeps you from seeing your grandchildren, Gincy thought. *A real shame.* And she wondered how her father had felt about Tommy's showing up without notice. Ed Gannon had probably just accepted the situation for what it was—inevitable.

Above all, be kind. If you can't change something, accept it and make lemonade.

"Has Tommy been looking for more work?" Gincy asked her mother. "When I was in town earlier, I saw several signs advertising low-skilled jobs. Full-time jobs at that."

"I don't like to ask him about work. Your brother is sensitive, Virginia."

"About as sensitive as a bucket of hair."

The second the words were out of her mouth, Gincy wanted to crawl under the table and stay there.

Tamsin put down her fork. "Mom, that's gross. We're trying to eat."

"Your mother has always had a rough way of speaking," Ellen said with a frown, poking at a carrot but not bringing it to her mouth.

And it got rougher whenever she was around her mother. Here she was, almost fifty years old, and still reacting childishly to her mother's well-known abhorrence of bad language and unpleasant imagery! Did people ever really grow up, Gincy wondered. Or were they always to some degree the silly or stubborn or fearful or insensitive kid they once were?

"Sorry, Mom," she said. "I shouldn't have said that." And she shouldn't have; what happened to setting a good example for her daughter? She remembered what Danielle had pointed out earlier. Her mother was going through a difficult time; she didn't need to be tormented or antagonized by her own daughter.

And what did Gincy really know about her brother? What had she ever really known, beyond the stereotype she had wanted or needed to see? For all she knew Tommy's apartment was plastered with posters of puppies and kittens and he cried himself to sleep every night after watching *It's a Wonderful Life*. And the fact was that he cared enough about his mother to have called his sister for help. That showed a heart in the right place.

Above all, Gincy thought, *be kind*.

"There's chocolate cake for dessert," she said. "The kind you like, Mom, with the white icing and the mint chips."

Ellen put down her fork, her meal almost untouched. "My appetite seems to be gone," she said. "Something seems to have killed it."

Tamsin reached across the table and took her grandmother's hand. "Come on, Grandma. I'm sure you could manage just a small slice. I'm having a piece."

"Well, all right. Just a small slice."

"But try to eat more steak first, okay, Grandma? You need your strength."

Gincy, only occasionally believing in God and usually only when convenient, thanked Him or Her or whatever God was, for the gift of her daughter.

CHAPTER 15

Gincy was sitting at the kitchen table, her legs stuck out in front of her, ankles crossed. Her mother had gone to her room, and Tamsin was somewhere in the house texting with her friend Julie. Gincy had given permission for this. It seems Julie had been asked out by their classmate Steven and couldn't decide whether she wanted to go out with him. Together the two girls were trying to guess what, exactly, "going out" meant at the moment and what, exactly, Julie was committing to if she said yes. "When in doubt," Gincy had told her daughter, "say no. Especially when it comes to boys."

"So, is it true what Grandma said, about your being boy crazy when you were my age?" Tamsin had asked.

"Absolutely not! My boy crazy phase came a lot later, long after I was out of the house and living on my own and a legal adult."

Tamsin had laughed. "I get the hint, Mom."

Gincy pressed the button on her phone that would connect her to her husband.

"It's been a weird day," she said when Rick answered his phone.

"Weird in what way?"

She told him first about her conversation with Danielle.

"Did she remind you to be nice?" Rick asked.

"Yes. And she told me to accept what can't be changed."

"Good advice."

"And she thanked us for the birthday check we sent Michelle."

"So far I'm not hearing anything that qualifies as weird," Rick said. "Or am I missing something?"

"No, this is the weird part." Gincy told her husband about running into Chrissy Smith and what her old friend had told her.

"Can you believe my parents held hands?" Gincy asked. "That they went for regular walks together? I know Chrissy isn't lying; why would she be? But why didn't Dad ever tell me that sort of thing?"

"Why would he have?" Rick asked. "Gincy, people don't usually relate the tiny private details of their daily lives. Think about it. Who else but you and I know that when we're alone we call each other Pinky and the Brain? If they did know they'd probably think we were nuts. Well, maybe we are nuts, obsessed with old cartoon characters. The point is, your dad was hardly the kind of guy to talk about something as personal as his marriage with his daughter. Or with anyone, for that matter."

"You're right," she said. "Pinky? I'm a mass of contradictions."

Rick laughed. "Brain, welcome to the human race."

"No really," she insisted. "On one hand, I never wanted my parents to be *unhappy*. But now that I think they might really *have* been happy, I'm . . . upset. What's wrong with me, Rick?"

"You're tired. This visit home is taking a bigger toll on

you than you expected. I should have come with you. I can be there tomorrow afternoon if you want."

"No, no, I'll be fine. But thanks."

"Did you see Tommy today?" Rick asked.

"No. It seems he comes and goes as he pleases. Mom doesn't seem to mind. Rick? Do you think Dad was embarrassed by Tommy?"

"I'm not sure it was in Ed Gannon's nature to be embarrassed by anyone, let alone his own flesh and blood. I know he loved Tommy. He never said as much, but I know it. Ed seemed to me to be one of those people who tell you more with their silence—and by their actions—than with their words."

"You're right," Gincy said. "Dad wasn't a judgmental man. I mean, he knew when someone was trouble, but he didn't punish or mock him for it. In fact, I remember there was a guy who worked at the hardware store once, a long time ago. He was nice but seriously incompetent, to the point of being a menace to the other guys. I remember there was an accident with the machine you made keys with. I was fascinated with that machine when I was a kid. Anyway, Dad gave this guy chance after chance. Finally, the store owner fired the guy. I really don't think Dad could bring himself to do it, even though as manager it was probably his responsibility."

And I really should have learned that lesson from my father, she thought. *Compassion. Patience. Above all, be kind.*

"And remember," Rick was saying, "as you yourself have pointed out, for all anyone knows, Tommy has mental issues or a learning disorder that was never identified. We can't judge him."

"I know. Rick, there's more." She went on to tell her

husband about her mother's distress while writing out her Christmas cards.

"Of course there was a reason she hadn't written out her cards yet," she said. "The idea was too painful for her. And what did I do? Force the issue."

"You meant well," Rick told her. "You tried to get her engaged in what was once a pleasant activity for her. That's all, Gincy."

"And poor Tamsin had to witness the debacle."

"Our daughter is a strong young woman. I'm sure she handled it."

I hope so, Gincy thought. "And then I ran into Adele Brown, you know, the woman at Number Twenty-one."

"Boy, you've had a busy day!"

"Tell me about it. Anyway, she told me how she and her husband have been concerned about Mom. About how they offered to call me but how my mother told them she was fine and not to call me because I was so busy with my big, important job in the city."

"Huh. Those were your mother's words? A big, important job?"

"According to Adele, but maybe she embellished. I've never known my mother to acknowledge that I do anything more important than sweep floors." Gincy sighed. "I'm sure all the while Adele was telling me about her concerns she was thinking what a lousy daughter I am, leaving her aged, grieving mother to rot away all alone in a dirty house."

Rick sighed. "I'm sure she was thinking no such thing. All right, I don't know the woman, maybe she was thinking just that, but you can't be concerned with other people's judgments. Just do what you think is the right thing. And that's exactly what you're doing. You're there in Appleville, with your mother."

"I should have come here before now," Gincy said. "I should have acted without waiting for someone to beg me to come home and help. I should have known Mom might be having trouble adjusting to widowhood. Why am I so insensitive when it comes to her? Why have I never been able to make the transition I made with Dad that summer I met you and Clare and Danielle? I couldn't wait to get on the road the moment Dad's funeral was over. You had to force me to go to that awful lunch at that awful restaurant afterward. And I know the funeral home recommended it, but it was still awful. Why didn't I *want* to stay around? Why didn't I *want* to make sure that Mom was okay?"

"Would it be too clichéd to say that the mother-and-daughter relationship is often fraught?"

"Yes," Gincy said. "It would. And look at Danielle and her mother, and Clare and hers. They get along beautifully. And Tamsin likes me, I know she does. I'm the freak show of the bunch."

"Gincy. Take a deep breath. Look, are you at all concerned about your mother continuing to live alone?" Rick asked. "Do you think she's competent, aside from the grieving, I mean?"

Gincy sighed. "I think she's competent, yes. I don't think she needs a minder, not full time. It's not time yet for us to be thinking about assisted living, as long as I can get her to eat regularly again and to show some interest in the house."

"Okay. Good. Try to keep focused on the task at hand, which is to get your mother through this phase. Try not to—now, don't freak out—try not to focus too heavily on your own feelings. Keep your thoughts on her."

"What did I do to deserve you?" Gincy asked suddenly.

Rick seemed to hesitate a moment before answering. "What do you mean?" Gincy thought he sounded wary.

"What's that song from *The Sound of Music*? It goes something like, 'Somewhere in my youth or childhood, I must have done something good.' To be loved by you, I mean."

Rick laughed. "Virginia Gannon-Luongo, you're getting sentimental in your old age."

"Are you calling me old?"

"Your middling age," Rick corrected.

"Yes," she said. "I am getting sentimental. And it's all because of you."

CHAPTER 16

"What about this one?" Tommy asked, holding out a screwdriver with black tape around the handle.

Gincy looked at it and shook her head. "Too big."

They were alone together in the part of the basement that had been their father's workspace. Ed Gannon had kept his tools carefully labeled and stored, the floor swept clean of all wood chips or metal shavings, and his copies of *Popular Mechanics* and *Woodworkers Guide* neatly stacked.

They were looking for a screwdriver of a particular size. Gincy had noted that the screws in several plates covering outlets on the first floor needed tightening. It was a job she could easily handle. At home, she, not Rick, was the one to change the lightbulbs and hang the pictures and fix the garbage disposal when it broke down because Rick had accidentally dropped a fork into it. Or the lid of a small metal can. He did that at least once a month.

"I've never been good with my hands," Tommy said, replacing the too-large screwdriver in its slot. "Not like Dad. He tried to teach me stuff but, I don't know, I never really got it." He ran a finger along the edge of the worktable. Gincy saw that his nail was ragged and there was a scar on the back of his hand. "Maybe I never really paid attention."

The tone of wistfulness and regret in her brother's voice struck Gincy powerfully. Certainly she had never heard it before, but maybe she simply hadn't been listening.

"Not everyone is good with his hands, Tommy," she said. "Rick is a menace around sharp objects but that doesn't make him any less valuable as a person."

Tommy smiled a bit.

"This should do." Gincy held up a screwdriver with a red plastic handle. And then something tucked at the very back of the worktable, against the rough basement wall, caught her eye.

"What's that?" Gincy asked.

"I'll show you." Tommy reached across the table and carefully drew toward them a lovely, partially carved oval frame.

"It's oak," Tommy explained. "Dad could tell what sort of tree a piece of wood came from just by looking at the grain. He tried to teach me that, too, but . . . Anyway, this was for Mom's grandmother's old mirror—you know, the one in her bedroom. The glass is okay, but the frame is cracked. Dad was replacing it for her but then he died. It wasn't a surprise or anything. Anyway, I wish I could finish it but . . ."

Gincy looked down at the intricate carvings of flowers and vines. It was a beautiful piece. And it was a typically kind gesture on the part of her father, and a romantic one, too. Replacing the frame was something only a husband who truly loved his wife would do for her. Like hold her hand when they went for walks.

"Dad meant everything to Mom," Tommy said, as if reading his sister's thoughts. "She relied on him totally. It

should have been Mom who died first. Dad was stronger. He
would have been okay. He wouldn't have forgotten to pay
the electric bill or to throw out the milk when it went bad."

Gincy shook her head. "Tommy, you're exaggerating.
All Mom did was criticize Dad, and he was only ever kind
to her."

"That's so not true," Tommy replied forcefully. "You
should have seen her all those times Dad went to visit you
in Boston. She hardly slept. She was worried he was going
to get mugged or killed in a car accident or pushed onto
the tracks in a T station. She worried he was going to eat
something weird that might make him sick. She worried
about *everything*. When he walked through the front door
she'd be like, beaming. And she always made him his favorite meatloaf the day he came home. And he always said
how glad he was to be here. He meant it, I know he did."

Gincy frowned down at her father's handiwork. Could
what Tommy was telling her be true? Could she really
have been so wrong about her mother's love for her father? Her parents holding hands. . . . The evidence certainly was piling up against her.

"You don't know everything, Gince," Tommy said,
more quietly now. "You're way smarter than me, but you
don't know everything."

"You're right, Tommy," she said. "I'm sorry."

"That's okay. I gotta go. I'm working at the convenience
store today. You know something, Gince? I like to work.
Didn't used to, but I do now." Tommy shrugged. "Funny
how things change."

Gincy smiled and watched her brother slip into his coat
and trudge up the basement stairs. The coat—so he did actually have one—was threadbare, as well as stained. She
wasn't sure it would survive a washing in her mother's old
machine at the other end of the basement. Her father's

winter parka was probably upstairs in the tiny front hall closet, but Ed had been a much bigger man than his son. There was no way Tommy could wear his father's coat and be comfortable. Gincy sighed. At least Tommy had a wool hat, even if it was a bit too small for his head and didn't quite cover his ears.

Suddenly in her mind's eye she saw her brother as a little kid in his big, puffy blue snowsuit with a long woolen scarf wound tightly around his neck. He had had such an adorable smile. What had happened to that innocent child? Everyone had promise of some sort when they started out in this life. What had happened to Tommy's promise?

Gincy shook off a powerful wave of sadness. It wasn't easy to do. Then she stuck the screwdriver in the back pocket of her jeans and went upstairs. Tighten the plates surrounding the electrical outlets first, and then start one of several loads of laundry.

CHAPTER 17

Before Gincy made lunch for her mother and daughter, she checked in with her assistant by phone. E-mail and texting were all well and good, but Gincy felt you could only get a really true sense of things via the human voice.

"Everything's fine here," Matt assured her in his usual brisk way. "Running like clockwork, your instructions being followed, deadlines being met. I'll send you Tim's draft of the feature story for the arts section later. In the meantime, you just enjoy your time with your mom."

Gincy resisted the urge to say, "Yes, sir!", thanked Matt for his efforts, and ended the call. She realized she had been half hoping for a crisis that would require her immediate presence back in Boston and felt a bit ashamed. Would she really have run off? No, she thought, of course not. Of course not.

Tamsin and Ellen came into the kitchen together.

"Hi, Mom. What are we having for lunch?" Tamsin asked.

"Ham and cheese sandwiches and chicken noodle soup. How does that sound, Mom?"

Ellen took her seat and unfolded her napkin before replying. "I'm sure it will be fine, Virginia. Though I saw you told Tommy to buy Progresso. I prefer Campbell's."

Gincy let the comment pass. "Mom," she said, "I was thinking. Why don't you come with me while I run a few errands after lunch? You really should take advantage of the weather before the big snows start. Fresh air is good for you. It will put apples in your cheeks."

"That's a funny expression," Tamsin said.

Ellen shook her head. "I think I'll stay home."

"We could stop at the library," Gincy suggested, unde-terred. "Maybe they have a new title in that mystery series you like, what's it called? The Bran Muffin Detectives or something?"

Tamsin rolled her eyes. "The Soufflé Sleuths, Mom."

"Well, I knew it had something to do with food."

"I haven't read one of those books since . . ." Ellen shook her head. "Well, it's been a long time."

"All the more reason we should go to the library, then. Maybe they'll have another mystery series you'd like. I'm sure the librarian can recommend something."

Ellen took a spoonful of soup before answering. "If you say so, Virginia. Tamsin, would you please pass the salt?"

Gincy hesitated, and then ventured on. "And if it's not too tiring for you, maybe we could take a stroll around that pond out by Margery Road. I doubt it's thoroughly frozen yet. There might still be some ducks. We could bring some bread for them."

Carefully, Ellen took her napkin from her lap and put it next to her plate and bowl. "On second thought," she said, "I think I'll stay home. I feel a little tired." Without another word she got up from the table and left the room. She had barely touched her lunch.

Gincy put her hand to her forehead and sighed. She had gone too far. What had she hoped for? That miraculously she and her mother would walk arm in arm around the pond in happy harmony, her mother confessing openly to her sadness and despair? And what would happen then? Gincy would be free to go back to Boston without guilt. . . .

"I'll wrap up the sandwich and put it in the fridge," Tamsin said.

Gincy gave her daughter a weak smile. "Thanks."

"You could stop by the library anyway, Mom, and get a few books for her. Maybe reading would help take her mind off things."

"I will. Would you mind staying here with Grandma?" Gincy asked. "Just to keep an eye on her. I'm sure she'll be fine but . . ."

Tamsin smiled. "Sure. And if she's hungry later I'll try to get her to eat the rest of her sandwich, and not just dessert."

"You're a good granddaughter, Tamsin."

"And you're a good daughter, Mom."

Gincy wished she could believe that.

Chapter 18

It was almost three o'clock in the afternoon. Tamsin, in her usual seemingly effortless way, had convinced her grandmother not only to finish her abandoned lunch but also to accept an offer of tea at Adele Brown's house. For all Gincy knew, it was the first time her mother had left the house in weeks. And given the fact that Ellen was not happy with Gincy's "poking around," as she put it, it was better she not be at home while her daughter got on with the cleaning, which is what Gincy was now doing.

She started in her parents' bedroom, vacuuming the small area rugs, one on either side of the bed, chasing months' worth of dust from the furniture, and washing the inside of the windows and the windowsills. She felt uncomfortable in the room, as if she were intruding upon, even violating, a private space. She wondered if all adult children felt that way about being in their parents' bedroom, that inner sanctum where parents once again became their private selves. She made a mental note to ask Danielle and Clare for their thoughts about that. Someday, when she had less pressing matters to deal with.

Gincy moved over to her mother's low dresser. Carefully

she wiped clean the old mirror that had once belonged to her great-grandmother. The frame was indeed badly cracked, and Gincy thought it odd that the glass hadn't broken, too. The frame was plain, unlike the intricately carved one her father had been crafting when he died. She wondered if her mother would have complained that the new frame wasn't exactly like the old one. She wondered if she would have appreciated the time and effort and skill her husband had put into creating the new frame.

Dresser dusted and polished, next she moved over to the bed and picked up the photo of her father from her mother's nightstand. It must have been taken when her father was in his early or midthirties. He was smiling, his hands on his hips. He was wearing a hat set at a jaunty angle. He looked, Gincy thought, very happy.

For the life of her she couldn't recall having seen this photo before. She wondered if her mother had put it out only after her father died. She remembered what Tommy had told her about her mother waiting eagerly for her father to come home from his visits to Boston. About Dad being the stronger of the two. How much of the truth of her parents' relationship had she ever really known? What had she wanted to see and what had she needed to believe? What, if anything, did her stubbornly held opinion of the union between Ellen and Ed Gannon have to do with reality?

It was then that Gincy noticed a thick book bound in black leather sitting on the lower shelf of the nightstand. It had the unmistakable look of a Bible. Several bookmarks protruded from the pages. She had no recollection of ever seeing a Bible in the house when she was growing up. In fact, it was only in college that she had ever done any serious reading from it, and that was more for historical and literary interest than for spiritual assistance. She knew that her mother had been a member of a local church for some time; the assistant pastor had conducted her father's funeral. Maybe someone at the Church of the Risen Lord had suggested she own a copy of what was arguably one of the most famous books in the world. And she wondered if her mother was able to take comfort in its words of wisdom.

Well, she wasn't going to ask her mother about her prayer habits. Not after she had been so ham-fisted by suggesting a walk around the pond, the scene of romantic strolls with her husband. But she was curious about the pages her mother had earmarked. She wondered if it would be wrong to open the book to those pages. After all, whatever she found might help her in some way to help her mother.

Putting all scruples about privacy aside, Gincy picked up the book and opened it to the first bookmarked page.

Psalm 23. No great surprise there, Gincy thought. The words of the psalm had probably helped millions of people through the centuries survive periods of sorrow and distress.

The Lord is my shepherd;
I shall not want.

She read on to the end.

Surely your goodness and mercy shall follow me all the days of my life
And I will dwell in the house of the Lord for ever.

She turned to another bookmarked page. And there, written in tiny careful letters next to a few lines of Psalm 34, Ellen had written: *Ed's favorite.*

Who among you loves life
and desires to enjoy prosperity?
Keep your tongue from evil-speaking
and your lips from lying words.
Turn from evil and do good;
seek peace and pursue it.
"Above all, be kind."

Gincy realized she had spoken those words aloud.

Did her mother read that psalm, her husband's favorite, every night before she turned off the lights? And when she did read the psalm, how much did she take its message to heart? Did she remember all of the good her husband had done in this world, before he had been called away? Well, if what Tommy had told her about their mother's devotion to their father was true, and why wouldn't it be, Ellen Gannon *did* remember all the good her husband had done.

Gincy closed the book and put it back on the lower shelf of the nightstand. Her throat was tight. She had seen enough.

CHAPTER 19

Ellen picked up the plastic bottle of milk and sniffed it warily. "One more day," she announced.

"But Mom," Gincy said, "we just opened the bottle yesterday."

"I know my milk. And in this house we fold the napkins in half, like a rectangle. Not into a triangle. You should know that, Virginia."

"Yes, Mom. How was tea at Mrs. Brown's?"

The three women were gathered in the kitchen about to settle down to dinner.

"She made these awesome cinnamon and sugar thingies," Tamsin said. "Like little spirals. I asked her for the recipe."

"Mom?" Gincy prodded.

"The tea was too strong. She lets it brew for too long. And speaking of too strong, I don't know how you drink that coffee you do."

"What coffee, Mom?"

"That leftover coffee from breakfast. It's going to rot your stomach."

Seek peace and pursue it, Gincy thought. Her father's favorite psalm.

"Still, it was nice of Mrs. Brown to have you over, wasn't it, Mom?" Gincy said.

Ellen nodded. "Yes, Virginia. The Browns have always been considerate neighbors."

"Our neighbors in Boston are weird," Tamsin said. Hurriedly, she added, "I mean in a good way. The people upstairs are performance artists. And the people downstairs, they're new, they moved in just last year, they're just regular artists. One's a painter and one does weaving. I have one of his scarves."

Ellen frowned. "What is a performance artist?"

While Tamsin struggled to explain this concept to her grandmother, Gincy thought again of the lovely oak frame her father had been working on when he died, and of Tommy's admitting that he wished he could finish his father's work. Poor Tommy. He had sounded almost wistful that morning, talking about their father. Tommy must miss him almost as much as their mother did. It was true she still hadn't come out and said, "I miss my husband," but maybe, Gincy thought, that was because she was afraid that the minute she did admit to missing him, the floodgates would open and she would fall totally apart and not be able to go on and . . .

No, Gincy thought, glancing at her mother's stern and frowning face. *Not Mom. No matter what Tommy thinks, Mom is tough.*

Except for when she wasn't. Except for when she needed support or guidance and looked to her Bible and to the words of her late husband's favorite psalm. Except for when she neglected to clean the bathroom and forgot to pay the electric bill. Except for when she couldn't find the emotional strength to go through her husband's belongings.

"Mom?" Gincy said when Tamsin had finished trying to explain the inexplicable to her grandmother. "If it's okay with you, I thought I'd go through those clothes of Dad's you said you wanted to give to the charity shop. Some might need airing out or washing before I bring them in."

Ellen took a sip from her glass before answering, and when she did, she looked not at her daughter but down at the remains of her meal. "The clothes are fine where they are, Virginia," she said.

"Are you sure? I could –"

"No." Ellen said firmly. "I said no. You never listen to me, Virginia."

Gincy winced. "Okay, Mom. Sorry."

The three women continued to eat in silence until Ellen suddenly asked how long Gincy and Tamsin were planning to stay.

Gincy didn't know how to answer that question. She had lied to her mother when she had told her she had come home for a Christmas visit when she had really come home to offer what help she could to a grieving woman. But now she wondered if she had been doing more harm than good, causing her mother pain instead of offering succor, forcing her to face things she simply wasn't yet ready to face. Was it really a good idea for her to linger on?

"Virginia, I asked you a question."

"Sorry," Gincy said, and she was. "My mind wandered. Not too long, Mom. Don't worry."

She had no idea if that had been the right thing to say.

"Grandma," Tamsin asked. "Would you like more stew?"

"Just a small spoonful, thank you. I'll help myself."

Gincy watched her mother lift the serving spoon from the bowl. Ellen's plain gold wedding ring was virtually embedded in her finger. Well, it would be. Gincy couldn't remember ever seeing her mother without it. She wondered if her father had been buried with his wedding ring. There had been an open coffin—Dad in his one good suit with his one good tie, a tie that Gincy had given him many Christmases ago—but for the life of her she couldn't remember noticing his wedding ring. Would her mother have asked the funeral director to remove it before the casket was closed so that she could take it home with her and keep it close? It was certainly not something Gincy felt she could ask her mother, not without sounding morbid. If Rick died before she did, she certainly would want—

"Virginia," Ellen said. "You're frowning. You'll get unbecoming wrinkles."

"I'm fifty. I already have unbecoming wrinkles."

"You should use face cream."

"We call it moisturizer these days, Mom," Gincy said, "and I do use it. And sunblock. I'm glad you liked the stew."

"Yes," Ellen said. "It was fine. Is there any of the chocolate cake left?"

Well, Gincy thought, *at least I made up for ruining her lunch earlier.* "Yes, Mom," she said. "There is."

When the stew had been consumed, Tamsin cleared away the plates and Gincy brought the cake to the table.

"Aren't you worried about Justin," Ellen asked suddenly, when she had finished the slice of cake Gincy had given her. "Living all alone in Connecticut?"

I wonder what brought that on, Gincy thought. Maybe

her mother was wondering about the whereabouts of her own son.

"He's not alone, Grandma," Tamsin said. "He has a roommate. And he lives in a nice part of Greenwich. Well, I think all parts of Greenwich are nice. It's really pretty."

"But he's so far away from his family. Aren't you concerned, Virginia?"

"Of course Rick and I are concerned, Mom," Gincy said. "We're concerned that he be happy and safe and that he enjoy what he's doing."

"But so far away from his family," her mother repeated. "How can you keep track of him?"

"He's twenty-five, Grandma," Tamsin said. Then she laughed. "I'm not so sure he wants us to be keeping track of him!"

"And I was alone in Boston all those years," Gincy pointed out. "From the age of seventeen. And I was fine."

And I was never lonely, she thought. *I never missed home, ever. I was fine being without them, Mom and Dad and Tommy. But maybe, just maybe, they weren't fine without me.*

"Have another piece of cake, Mom," she said abruptly, dismissing the painful thought.

But instead of replying to this suggestion, Ellen moved her plate aside and poked at the tablecloth with her forefinger. "This cloth is sticky," she said.

"I know. I was thinking that maybe I—I mean, that you might want to replace it," Gincy said. "I've tried to clean it but . . ."

"You're not trying hard enough, Virginia. What it needs is some serious elbow grease."

"Yes, Mom," Gincy said.

"Your father always believed in elbow grease. He always said, when you think you can't get a job done properly, just apply some elbow grease."

Tamsin looked from her mother to her grandmother. "What's elbow grease?" she asked warily. "It's not really made of elbows, is it?"

For the first time since she had been home, Gincy saw her mother smile.

CHAPTER 20

Gincy and Tamsin were cleaning up after dinner. Ellen, sated from second helpings of stew and cake, was in the living room dozing in front of the television.

"Grandma seems better," Tamsin said, stacking dry plates into the cupboard. "Not as sad as when we first got here."

"Do you think so?" Gincy asked. "I'm of two minds about that. She's grieving, she must be, but she either can't or won't admit it. She's hardly mentioned Grandpa, but she must be thinking of nothing else but him. I worry that if she continues to keep her feelings all bottled up, she'll never really heal."

Tamsin shrugged. "When we had that grief counseling at school—remember, after that senior committed suicide right before graduation last year?—the guy said that grief takes as many forms as there are people. Some people scream and cry and some people retreat into themselves. And some people pretend the bad thing never happened. He said you have to let people grieve in their own way."

"I know. He was right. Hey, you know what my old class-mate Chrissy Smith told me the other day? That Grandma and Grandpa used to walk by the pond out by Margery Road every Saturday afternoon. And that they held hands."

Tamsin put her hand to her heart. "How sweet! Wow."

"That's why I suggested Grandma and I go there this af-ternoon," Gincy confessed. "I had some silly notion that if I took her to the pond she might open up."

"It wasn't silly, it was nice, Mom. You meant well."

"You know what they say about the road to Hell, don't you? That it's paved with good intentions."

"Language is weird," Tamsin said, putting the last of the silverware away. Then she sank into her chair at the table. "You know, Mom, like I said, Grandma and I had an okay time at Mrs. Brown's. Grandma and Mrs. Brown seem to like each other well enough, but I don't think they're close at all. I mean, they call each other 'Mrs.' And Mrs. Brown is a lot younger than Grandma."

"People of varying ages can be good friends," Gincy said. She dried her hands on a kitchen towel, noting as she did that it was ripped and should be tossed. Her mother had always had a thing about using kitchen towels until they were literally rags.

"I know that. It's just that I was thinking. Grandma has always seemed *so* old. Do you know what I mean? Grandpa didn't seem old to me at all, even though he was seventy-eight when he died. I think it must be a personal-ity thing."

Gincy thought about this for a moment. "You know something," she said then. "You're right. It's like my mother was born an old woman. Maybe it *is* a personality thing."

"And I was thinking about something else," Tamsin

said. "Doesn't Grandma have any friends? Didn't she and Grandpa ever hang out with another couple? She seems so alone and isolated. Her phone hasn't rung once since we've been here. Isn't there anyone in town who cares?"

Gincy shook her head and joined her daughter at the table. "Honestly, I don't know the answers to those questions. I vaguely recall a woman my mother used to spend time with, I think her name was Sally, but that was years ago. And as far as a couple, no one comes to mind. I should ask Tommy. He might know of someone I could contact, someone who might be able to check in on her when we're back in Boston."

"Grandma doesn't like to ask for help," Tamsin declared. "She's just like you, or I guess I should say you're just like her. And if you don't ask for help, how is anyone going to know that you need it, unless you're, like, bleeding from the eyes or something else totally obvious?"

Gincy smiled at her daughter. "You're one very smart cookie, Tamsin Luongo. I'm glad you're here for Grandma, and for me. Thank you. But Tamsin, you know you could go home at any time. I could put you on a bus back to Boston, or Dad could come and pick you up. You could be spending your Christmas vacation with your friends, goofing off. After all, you work so hard when school's in session, I hate to see you whiling away what little free time you have here in Appleville."

"It's okay, Mom," Tamsin said. "I've got almost three weeks off. There's plenty of time to hang out when we get back home. Besides, I've got my iPhone. When Grandma gets too grumpy, I just play a game or something."

"Or you read the biography you're supposed to be reading, right?"

"That too."

"By the way, what did Julie decide about going out with that guy, Steven?"

Tamsin laughed. "She decided he wasn't smart enough for her. But she didn't tell him that. She let him down nicely."

"Above all, be kind," Gincy said. "It's not a bad way to live. Now, let's get Grandma to bed."

CHAPTER 21

"Gincy. Hi. So, tell me."

"No," Gincy said. "I've been selfish since I've been here. I want to know how *your* day was."

"Uneventful," Rick told her. "Work is fine, the loft is fine, I've got a new craft beer to try and I'm hoping it's more than just fine, and Justin says he's looking forward to being with his family at Christmas. And yes, I watered the tree."

"Great. Okay, now it's my turn."

And Gincy told her husband what Tommy had shared with her about her parents' relationship, about how her mother depended on her father, about how she missed Ed when he was off in Boston, about the lovely frame he had been carving for his wife when he died.

"I'm struggling, Rick," she said. "I'm trying to figure it all out. How can Tommy's truth square with what I say is true?"

"One family, multiple truths. That's always the way it is, Gincy."

"Yeah, but . . . The thing is, Dad never said a word against my mother. He wouldn't. He was a gentleman. But

Mom criticized Dad all the time, and to anyone who would listen—the neighbors, the aunts and uncles, even the mailman."

Rick laughed. "The mailman?"

"Okay, maybe not the mailman. But it never stopped, Rick. She complained that Dad couldn't replace a broken bicycle spoke, which by the way was a lie because he was the one who taught me how to replace a broken bicycle spoke. She complained that he didn't stand up straight. Well, what did she expect? The man spent a lifetime lifting and hauling stuff in that hardware store, boxes of nails and lawn mowers and huge power saws. Is it surprising he was a little stooped? He didn't stand up straight because he couldn't! She complained he always forgot when it was time for a haircut. Why should he have bothered to remember? Mom was the one who told him when to go to the barber. She would even hand him the five dollars or whatever it cost and send him on his way, like he was a little kid. How can you always be criticizing someone you love?"

"First," Rick said, "maybe your mother simply wasn't able to show her love in any other way. Okay, I know that sounds crazy, but not everyone is comfortable expressing their feelings. It makes them feel too vulnerable."

"But what about how poor Dad felt?" Gincy insisted.

"Maybe he blocked all of it out, the chatter, the complaining. A lot of people learn to do that. Men, mostly, but that's just my opinion. Anyway, I'm not saying it's the healthiest way to go through life, but if it works . . ."

"That's not what you're doing, is it?" Gincy asked worriedly. "Blocking me out because I'm so annoying?"

"Gincy. No, it is not at all what I'm doing."

Gincy sighed. "I know. Sorry. It's just that, I always thought Dad was unhappy. I mean, when I started to think about him at all, and that wasn't until the summer I met you. But maybe I was wrong. Maybe I was projecting my own dissatisfactions with Mom and life in Appleville onto him. I thought that if I was unhappy here, he must have been, too."

"It wouldn't be the first time someone's been blinded by her own prejudice."

"Yikes. When you put it like that, it sounds almost criminal. Rick? Did Dad ever talk to you about Mom?"

"Never," Rick said. "But I always got a strong sense that he was devoted to her. If he wasn't exactly happy, and I'm not saying he wasn't, then he wasn't exactly unhappy, either."

"All those time he stayed with us in Boston, I never once remember him calling Mom. Or her calling him, for that matter. And we know he refused to have a cell phone, so he wasn't chatting with her at midnight after we had all gone to bed."

"I don't think that generation of married couples went in much for phone conversations," Rick said. "For one, they were never apart for that long. I bet your father talked to your mother via the phone fewer than ten times in their life together."

"Huh," Gincy said. "That's an interesting point. Before Dad started to visit us, they were never apart for even a night, not that I can remember. It's not like he had to travel for work or she had any relatives she wanted to visit across the country. But wouldn't that mean they would be so lonely for each other when Dad was in Boston and Mom back home that they would spend hours on the phone?"

Rick sighed. "Remember, Gincy, no one knows what goes on in a marriage but the two people in it."

"I know. Mom asked me how long I was staying."

"Good question. What did you say?"

"I said something like, not too long, don't worry."

"What did she say?" Rick asked.

"Nothing."

"You'll just have to play it by ear then."

"I'm going to talk to Mom about money tomorrow," Gincy told him. "I'm going to ask to see her checkbook."

Rick whistled. "Good luck," he said. "That's going to be unpleasant. Your mother is a proud woman. Remember the fuss she made back when your dad died and we asked to see her financials to be sure she had enough to pay for the funeral and all?"

"I vaguely remember her calling me a rapacious vulture after her fortune. Well, rapacious is my addition."

Rick laughed. "I hate to tell you, but she said a lot more once you'd left the room."

"I don't want to know! Rick? I love you."

"I love you, too, Gincy," he said. "Sleep well."

"I'll try," she promised. "But it's not so easy without you."

CHAPTER 22

Gincy was stirring soup on the one working burner on the stove. Tamsin was setting the kitchen table for lunch, folding the napkins into rectangles, not triangles. Ellen, showing a welcome interest in the upkeep of her home, was rubbing at an invisible spot on the edge of the sink with a sponge. Well, it was invisible to Gincy, but Ellen swore it was there and was applying a good deal of elbow grease to it. Tamsin had been glad to know that "elbow grease" was just an expression, though she had told her mother she still couldn't understand how hair would have gotten into a bucket.

Tommy was in the living room setting up the artificial Christmas tree. It was the same tree the family had when Gincy and Tommy were small. Gincy was surprised it hadn't disintegrated long ago. Maybe, she thought, it was made of some super material that would outlast them all, even if that meant spending its final century in a landfill.

Her brother appeared now in the doorway of the kitchen, holding something spindly, green, and faded. "I've got one extra branch," he said. "I can't figure out where it goes.

Dad never had a branch left over when he put up the tree."

"I'm sure it doesn't matter," Tamsin said. "Anyway, he had lots of practice."

Tommy stared down at the branch in his hand, as if he weren't quite sure how it had gotten there, and then propped it against the wall in a corner of the kitchen and joined the others, now gathered at the table.

"Grandma," Tamsin asked. "What made you marry Grandpa?"

Ellen frowned. "What a silly question. I was in love with him, of course. Why else would I have married the man?"

Tamsin turned to her mother. "That's why you married Dad, right, Mom? Because you loved him."

"Yes," Gincy said. "And because I liked him. You can love someone but not really like them very much."

Is that how I feel about Mom, Gincy wondered. *I love her, but I don't very much like her?* But how can you like or dislike someone if you don't really *know* her? Sometimes, Gincy thought, Ellen Gannon seemed like a complete stranger. She thought of the Bible in her mother's bedroom. More than sometimes.

"Don't talk nonsense, Virginia," Ellen said in that dismissive, definitive tone Gincy knew so well. "If you love someone, of course you also like them, end of story."

Tommy slurped his soup. "Sorry," he said.

When the soup bowls and plates had been cleared, Gincy brought tea and cookies to the table.

"I know the cookies look kind of weird," Tamsin said. "I guess I'm just not used to your oven, Grandma. But they taste okay, I promise."

Tommy, who had already consumed two, nodded and gave his niece a thumbs-up.

"That oven is whacky," Tamsin whispered to Gincy. "Did you hear the noise it makes when it's heating up? It's like it's crying or something."

Gincy hid a grin and glanced across the table at her mother. Now seemed as good a time as any to bring up a difficult subject. Even more than music, food often soothed the soul of the savage beast, and her mother had eaten all of her lunch, including three of Tamsin's lopsided sugar cookies. "Mom," she said, "I'd like to take a look at your financial situation. Just to be sure everything is as it should be."

"You saw all that when your father died," Ellen said sharply.

"Yes, but that was six months ago. I'd like to be sure nothing's changed significantly or for the worse. So I'd like to see the bank statements. And your checkbook."

Ellen let her spoon drop into her mug of tea. "Are you saying I can't handle my own life?" she challenged.

Tommy cleared his throat. "Mom," he said, "just let her see the stuff, okay? She's smart."

"And I'm not?" Ellen demanded.

"Come on, Mom." Tommy's tone was gentle. "You forgot to pay the electric bill last month. Just let Gincy check up on stuff."

Ellen Gannon's face turned alarmingly red. "You promised you wouldn't tell your sister about that. Why did you have to go advertising my personal business?"

Gincy glanced at her brother. Tommy looked decidedly uncomfortable, almost frightened.

"He wasn't advertising it, Mom," she said. "He was worried about you. He did the right thing in telling me."

"Everyone forgets to do something important at one time or another, Grandma," Tamsin said. "It's normal.

Last week I forgot to brush my teeth one night before going to bed!"

"I forget to brush my teeth at night all the time," Tommy blurted.

Hence, the missing tooth, Gincy thought. "Mom, the papers."

"What does Richard say about this?" Ellen demanded. "Does he know what you're doing?"

"Yes," Gincy said calmly, "Rick knows what I'm doing and he agrees that it's right."

Ellen pushed away from the table. "All right then. If Richard thinks it's a good idea, you can see the papers. But I'm not happy about this one little bit."

She was back a moment later with a faded manila folder. She dropped it onto the table, narrowly missing upsetting the plastic saltcellar.

"I'm going to my room to lie down," she said. "I suddenly don't feel very well. That tuna salad you made, Virginia, had too much mayonnaise. And the soup was cold."

"I don't think you can get sick from cold soup," Tommy said, when Ellen had left the kitchen again. He looked concerned. "But maybe you can get sick from eating too much mayonnaise."

"Grandma's just being grumpy," Tamsin assured him. "She's not really sick. Can I be excused, Mom?"

"Sure."

Tamsin, already tapping at her iPhone, left the room.

Gincy turned to her brother. "Thanks, Tommy, for stepping in with Mom. I really appreciate your help."

Tommy smiled. "Yeah, sure. Look, Gince, what I said the other day, when you first came home, that Mom hates you. She doesn't hate you. I don't know why I said that. She doesn't really mean all the stuff she says. Like the way she's always telling you that you did something wrong. She did that with Dad, too, but she totally loved him. It's just the way she is."

Gincy was touched. Her brother was indeed a far more sensitive person than she had ever given him credit for. She remembered all the nasty comments she had made about him in the past, and if she were prone to blushing she would have blushed. "Thanks again, Tommy," she said. "And just for the record, I meant it when I said that I don't hate Mom."

"You know," Tommy said, and his tone sounded almost surprised, as if the thought was occurring to him for the first time. "I've never hated anyone, not even that guy I knew once from Roy's Tavern, the guy who broke into my place and stole a bunch of cash. He got caught, that's how I know it was him."

"Tommy," Gincy said, her hand to her heart, "that's awful. I'm sorry. I'm so glad you weren't home at the time. You could have been hurt."

Tommy shrugged. "And I didn't even hate Kate, when she left me. I mean, I kind of deserved that, I guess. Still I didn't hate her for getting a divorce." He smiled sadly. "She probably hated me."

"If she did, I'm sure she's long past that now, Tommy," Gincy said, hoping that it was the truth and that Kate, who was a nice person, had found someone more suitable to marry. "I wouldn't let it worry you."

"I don't. Not much. Look, how long are you staying?"

"I'm not sure," she admitted. "Tommy? Does Mom have any friends? Did she and Dad spend time with a particular couple? It seems that she's so alone."

Tommy toyed with the knife beside his plate. "I don't think Mom and Dad ever went in much for friends. I mean, I never knew about any." He looked up at his sister and gave her a rueful smile. "But maybe they just wanted to keep me away from people they liked."

Before Gincy could respond with a strong denial of such a thing, Tommy got up from the table. "I gotta go," he said. "Mr. Barone at the convenience store told me to come by this afternoon. He's getting a big shipment of something. Diapers, I think he said. Or maybe it was cat food."

"Take care, Tommy," Gincy said. "Do you wear one of those supports for the lower back? The kind Dad wore?"

Tommy shook his head.

"Maybe you should consider one, if you do a lot of lifting."

Tommy nodded. "Thanks, Gince."

And then he was gone.

Tommy was a lot like their father, Gincy thought, listening to the awful sound of his old truck starting up and pulling away from the house. He didn't make it a habit of speaking ill of people, even the ones who had hurt him. Maybe it hadn't always been that way with him, but did that matter? What mattered was Tommy in the here and now.

Gincy sighed. Poor Tommy. Thinking that his parents had purposely kept him at a distance from their friends, if any friends had indeed existed.

Seek peace and pursue it. As Rick had pointed out, it would never have crossed Ed Gannon's mind to be ashamed of his son. Or, Gincy thought, her mother's mind, either.

Gincy cleared away the tea things and opened the faded manila file. It didn't take long to go through its contents. It was all pretty straightforward; her mother had virtually no investments, a small retirement account, and a manageable mortgage. And she found nothing amiss, no bills unpaid and the checking account balanced to within a penny. There was no evidence of money going out to her brother, but that didn't mean her mother wasn't giving him small sums in cash from her weekly housekeeping budget. There would be no trace of that sort of thing. Still, what she had found overall was a huge relief. As soon as possible she would talk to Rick about how they could keep an eye on things going forward. And about how they could ensure that Tommy would be okay when Ellen passed. It had never occurred to Gincy to worry about her brother's future.

Better late than never, she thought. *Right, Dad?*

CHAPTER 23

Tamsin was keeping her mother company while she prepared dinner. Life on Crescent Road, Gincy thought, at least for the moment, had come down to a cycle of breakfast, lunch, and dinner, followed once again by breakfast, lunch, and dinner. Eat. Repeat. But with a seventy-eight-year-old depressed woman who needed encouragement to eat and a house that had been let go to clean and organize, there wasn't much time for fun and games.

Not that Ellen Gannon had ever been one for fun and games. Not as far as Gincy knew.

"Why did you ask your grandmother why she married your grandfather?" Gincy asked, searching for a slotted spoon in a drawer crowded with too many cheap cooking utensils.

Tamsin shrugged. "I guess I thought that maybe she would open up a bit. Talk about how she's feeling, about missing Grandpa. But she didn't, did she?"

"She was never one to talk about feelings. Opinions? She's always been full of those and ready to share them with anyone within earshot. Not so much feelings."

Tamsin laughed. "Sorry," she said. "I shouldn't laugh,

but when Grandma and I were alone before, she told me for like the millionth time that she missed out on having Appleville's first baby of the new year because you were so stubborn and refused to come out."

"See what I mean?" Gincy said, grinning. "Opinions. Anyway, I don't think I had much of a choice about coming out or staying in."

"You know what I was thinking about last night, before I fell asleep?"

"No."

"I was thinking about the time when you and Dad went away for a weekend to celebrate your anniversary. I think I was seven or eight and, remember, I stayed here with Grandma and Grandpa."

Gincy smiled. "I do remember that. Your father and I went to Newport. We had dinner that Saturday night at a restaurant that's been around since the seventeenth century. We had beef Wellington. It was one of the best meals I've ever eaten."

"Well *we* went to the ice-cream parlor after dinner one night," Tamsin said. "Grandma didn't want Grandpa and me to order the Kitchen Sink. She said that we'd never finish it and that it was a shameful waste of money. That's the word she used, shameful. I remember it because I'd never heard it before, and later on I had to ask Justin what it meant. Anyway, Grandpa went ahead and ordered it. Have you ever had the Kitchen Sink, Mom? You'd totally remember if you did."

Gincy shook her head. "I guess the answer is no."

"It's a gigantic bowl with a bunch of ice-cream scoops— vanilla, chocolate, and strawberry, and maybe coffee, I can't remember—with chocolate and caramel sauce and whipped cream, and nuts, and bananas. And they sprinkle all these tiny plastic animals in it. The waiters brought it to the table on something like a stretcher, and they sang some song, I forget what, and people clapped. Oh, yeah, and there were sparklers. Anyway, Grandpa and I dug in—they give you these special, really long spoons, I mean the handles are long—and eventually Grandma pushed aside the bowl of vanilla ice cream she had ordered and joined in."

"Grandma joined in?" Gincy asked. She was more than a little dubious. "I mean, I know she loves to eat, but the Kitchen Sink? That sort of mess is far more my kind of thing. Are you sure you're remembering that correctly?"

"Absolutely. It was so much fun. We all laughed like crazy. Grandma lined up all the little plastic animals we found in the bowl and said that they were on parade because they were celebrating your anniversary, yours and Dad's. I'd never seen her like that. So . . . How can I put it? So happy?"

Gincy shook her head. "You never told me that story. Why?"

Tamsin shrugged. "I didn't? I guess I thought that I had. Anyway, now you know."

Yes, Gincy thought. *Now I know.*

"Is Tommy coming back tonight?" Tamsin asked.

"No idea," Gincy answered. But she thought it would be nice if he did.

"Mom? I was thinking. Why doesn't Uncle Tommy move back in here with Grandma? She's lonely and he has so little money. And I know he's not seeing anyone, because I asked him. In fact, it was kind of sad what he said, that those days were over, like he's given up on being in love. Anyway, it seems like the perfect plan for Tommy and Grandma to live here together."

"The idea has occurred to me, too," Gincy admitted. "But I don't think it's as simple as all that. First, Grandma might not want him here. She might worry that he'd turn out to be a burden rather than a help around the house. And I'm not saying anything bad about your uncle, Tamsin. Just that he's not used to being needed and relied upon, and Grandma's not used to asking for his help. Living together might really damage their relationship."

"But what if Grandma *does* want him to come home?" Tamsin pressed.

Gincy sighed. "I've thought about that, too. And I don't know, I suspect that Tommy needs what little independence he's been able to forge for himself. He was a boy in this house, until he moved out, and that was a long time coming. Moving back home now . . . it might feel as if he had suddenly become an old man. It might feel as if the cycle of his life had come full turn, that his life was in some way over. It might damage his pride. Do you see what I mean?"

"Sort of. But it's just guessing, isn't it? We don't know what Grandma or Uncle Tommy feel about living here together, do we?"

"No," Gincy admitted. "We don't. We don't really know much at all."

CHAPTER 24

Gincy had made pork chops with applesauce and buttered egg noodles for dinner. Her father had loved that meal, something she hadn't remembered until the pork chops were almost done. She hoped her mother wouldn't be upset by the memories the meal might bring. It was hard to know what might set a person who was grieving so privately into a downward spiral. If you went around tearing your hair and crying out, "Another pork chop will never cross my lips!" a person would be pretty sure not to serve you a pork chop.

"Are you finished snooping through my papers?" Ellen asked, spooning applesauce onto her plate.

"I wasn't snooping," Gincy said. Her mother had really eaten the Kitchen Sink? "You gave them to me."

"Against my will."

Gincy saw Tamsin give her a warning look. She thought about the parade of little plastic animals. Fun and games. *Above all, be kind.*

"Well, to answer your question," she said, "yes, I have finished. The file is over there on the counter, next to the toaster oven."

"Where it's likely to catch fire!"

"The toaster oven isn't plugged in, Grandma."

"Well, it should be. Who unplugged it? And did you find anything wrong?" Ellen demanded. "Did I mislay thousands of dollars or forget to pay another bill?"

"Nothing's wrong that I can see. You've been doing a fine job of it all, Mom."

Ellen looked smug. "I told you so. Tommy never should have told you about that electric bill. He promised."

"But then we wouldn't have come to see you," Tamsin said. Hurriedly she added, "I mean, we would have come anyway, because it's Christmas. You are glad we're here, aren't you, Grandma?"

"Yes, Tamsin," she said, slicing a piece of pork chop. "I'm glad you're here. This pork chop is very tasty, Virginia."

Gincy smiled. "How do you like that book I brought home from the library?" she asked. "The new mystery series, the one about the ladies who sell crepes from a food truck and solve crime along the way. Where's it set? Seattle, I think."

"I haven't started to read it yet."

"Have you met any nice women at your church, Grandma?" Tamsin asked.

Ellen didn't look up from her meal. "Of course there are nice women at church."

"That's not really what Tamsin asked," Gincy said.

"What I mean is do you see any of them outside of church, like for lunch or to play cards or bingo or something?"

"Some of the ladies meet for bridge once a week," Ellen said, "but it doesn't interest me."

"Bridge?" Gincy asked, thinking of her earlier conversation with Tommy about their parents' social life. "Or the women?"

"Will you pass the noodles, Tamsin?" Ellen asked.

Tamsin did.

"Mom? What ever happened to that friend of yours, Sally something?"

Ellen looked puzzled. "Sally?"

"Yes, you remember," Gincy said. "The woman you used to go to the movies with. She had red hair."

"Oh," Ellen said. "Sarah. Virginia, that was years and years ago! Sarah and her husband were divorced when you were about fifteen. She moved to Concord to live with her sister."

"Do you keep up with her, Grandma?" Tamsin asked.

Ellen frowned. "No. I'm afraid it's not that easy to stay in touch with people when they move away. . . ."

"But there's the phone," Tamsin said. "And now there's e-mail and texting and Facebook. There are all sorts of ways you can be in touch with people!"

"Your grandmother doesn't have a computer," Gincy pointed out. "Or an iPhone."

"And I don't have any interest in either one," Ellen said firmly.

Tamsin opened her mouth, no doubt to offer another helpful suggestion, but Gincy silenced her with a small shake of her head. To Gincy at least, the message was clear. Ellen Gannon had chosen to isolate herself since her husband's death, and perhaps, as Tommy thought might be the case, even before that, at least to some extent. And that was understandable, if her husband had been her best friend. A husband who was his wife's best friend would be impossible to replace, and it would work the other way around, too. Ellen and Ed Gannon can't have been the only couple to find in each other's companionship all, or almost all, of what they needed from other people.

Is that the case with Rick and me, Gincy wondered? *Are we perhaps too closely bound together? If Rick were to die, would I survive on my own?*

Gincy felt her hand tighten around her fork. It didn't bear thinking about.

"Virginia?"

"Yes, Mom," she said.

"What have you brought in for dessert?"

Gincy was very glad for the change of subject.

"We have ice cream," she said. "Two flavors, chocolate and maple walnut. You could have a scoop of each, if you like."

Ellen Gannon frowned and lowered her fork. "Who ever heard of such a thing, two different flavors of ice cream together?"

Tamsin found a sudden need to bury her face in her napkin. Her shoulders began to shake suspiciously.

"I wouldn't serve you both scoops in the same bowl," Gincy said, eyes wide.

Her mother resumed her meal. "Well," she said. "I should hope not."

CHAPTER 25

"I miss you."

"Me too," Rick said. "I hate it when we're not to-gether. Everything feels—wrong."

"I hate it, too. It's a good thing we both feel the same way. I'm sure there are lots of couples who actually enjoy time apart."

"Ugh," Rick said. "Call me old-fashioned, but I'd rather be with my wife than without her, even when she's in one of her cantankerous moods."

"Me? Cantankerous?" Gincy laughed. "Never. By the way, have you been watering the tree? You know how quickly it will get dry."

"I've been watering the tree."

"Good." And that important fact ascertained, she lis-tened while her husband recounted the events of his day.

"We got snow," he told her. "Not much, a few inches, but enough to make the Gardens and the Commons look beautiful. Well, more beautiful."

"And work is all right?" she asked. "And your health? You haven't caught a cold or anything? You haven't fallen on the ice?"

"I'm happy to report that work is fine and so am I. Same as I was yesterday at this time. Don't worry about me, Gincy. Okay, your turn."

"I went through Mom's finances. Well, I snooped. That's her word. And everything is in order. The forgotten electric bill seems to have been a lone incident."

"Good," Rick said. "So we can put that concern aside for the moment."

"Not so fast. I still haven't asked about what financial help Mom might be giving Tommy." Gincy sighed. "I don't know, Rick. Maybe that's something you could handle, if you feel comfortable about it. I mean, maybe you could talk to Tommy about his financial situation. I don't want to embarrass him any more than I probably already did when I asked him the other night if he needed money. He said no, by the way. And if I ask Mom what she's been doing for Tommy, I'm pretty sure she'll stalemate."

"I'll do what I can to help, of course," Rick said. "We do need to know."

"Thank you, Rick," Gincy said. "I mean it. And there's something else I need to talk about."

"I'm listening."

"Earlier, when I was going through Mom's checkbook, it kind of startled me to see my father's name on the checks. Well, of course his name is there. Mom doesn't write that many checks and it'll be a while before she goes through the supply she has. But it's disturbing when you come across the vestiges of a life that's over, isn't it?"

"It is," Rick agreed. "I've told you about that first year after Annie passed. Memories assault you from so many places at once, it feels like a miracle that you're still standing. It was a good thing I had Justin to focus on. That helped me get through more than anything else could."

Gincy sighed. "Oh, Rick, you know all about grieving. The voice on the answering machine. The mail that keeps coming, addressed to someone no longer there to receive it. I found a flyer from Home Depot addressed to my father this morning and threw it out before Mom could see it. Anyway, it's disturbing, and yet you don't want those vestiges to be wiped away. It's like, as long as my father's name is on the checks, as long as his shirts are hanging in the bedroom closet and not given to the charity shop—by the way, I talked to Mom about passing them on, but she's having none of it—anyway, as long as Dad's worktable is set up in the basement and his old copies of *Popular Mechanics* are still there, he isn't entirely gone. It doesn't make sense, but that's the way it is."

"I'm sorry it's so difficult," Rick said gently. "Being there in that house. But I'm afraid there's no way it couldn't be difficult. And this experience, of being the survivor, comes to each one of us at some point in time. Well, to most of us."

"I know. I just keep thinking of what my mother must be feeling, every single moment of every single day. A terrible longing. Emptiness. How does she pass the hours knowing that her husband is never coming home, that they'll never share the same bed, that he'll never accompany her to church on Sundays, that he'll never even walk down the aisle of the grocery store with her? Do you think that's one reason Mom has been avoiding shopping for food? Because it reminds her too much of the comfortable daily life she shared with Dad?"

"I think it's possible, Gincy, yes. Memories are everywhere, even in the bread aisle."

"How is she even managing to put one foot in front of the other," Gincy went on, "day after lonely day? It's not like she has a child to care for, like you did with Justin, someone on whom she can focus her love and attention. Even Tommy's got a life of his own. Sometimes she doesn't see him for days on end."

Rick sighed. "The human spirit is strong. The will to live is primal. People go on. I don't know exactly how it works, Gincy. I wish I did."

"Me too. Rick, don't die, okay?"

"Uh, okay. I mean, I'm not planning on it any time soon."

"Good. I'll try not to die, either. I mean, before I'm really old."

"Well, now that we have that settled," Rick said, "tell me, is your mother any worse than when you got there?"

"Well, she still won't say anything directly about missing Dad, but she's definitely better than she was a few days ago." Gincy laughed. "Now that she has me to kick around."

"I'm going to float an idea here, Gincy, and I want you to consider it. I think your mother needs you. I think she's glad you're back home. And I think the only way she can express herself with you, for whatever wacky reasons, is by criticizing and being a curmudgeon, kind of like what she did with your father."

"That's insane!" Gincy cried. "Need me?" she said in a lower voice. "She's never needed me."

"Are you so sure about that?"

"Yes," Gincy said. "It's crazy. You need someone so you drive her away by your negativity? That's pretty much what she did with me, right from the start."

Well, Gincy thought, not right from the start. No, she could remember—when she allowed herself to remember—feeling genuinely close to her mother when she was a little girl. Memories of those early years had become painful to recall as time went by and she and her mother grew further apart, but she knew that if she gathered her courage she could face the memories and appreciate the warm relationship she and her mother had once shared. The picnics together in Appleville Park, just the two of them, sitting on the old plaid blanket, eating bologna sandwiches and drinking lemonade. Going to the movies together on a Saturday afternoon and treating themselves to a box of Raisinets. Her mother holding on to the seat of Gincy's first two-wheeled bike as she taught her daughter how to ride. Baking cupcakes for the school bake sales. It had all been so fun. So simple. So comforting.

But everything had started to change when Gincy had gone to high school. Why? Why had her mother become so critical and dismissive of her? And why had she, Gincy, allowed herself to become the same toward her mother?

"Gincy? Are you there?"

"Sorry," she said. "I was just thinking about the past. And about the notion of my mother needing me. It's just so hard to believe."

"Look, you're back there now, aren't you? You chose to go back, and she hasn't asked you to leave. She's even re-lying on you, isn't she, to make the meals. She's letting you clean her house. She made a fuss I'm sure, but she did actually let you see her finances. I'm no psychiatrist, but isn't it at least possible that she's happy you're there with her? Since when do human beings make sense?"

"Since never," Gincy admitted. And at dinner Ellen *had* said that she was glad Gincy and Tamsin were visiting, although that might have been a lie for Tamsin's sake.

But Gincy had never known her mother to be a liar, in spite of the few recent incidents, and obviously her mother had felt she had good reasons for keeping certain bits of information from her daughter. If anything, the Ellen Gannon Gincy knew could be brutal in telling the truth as she saw it.

Rick yawned. "Sorry," he said. "It's not the company."

"You're tired. I'll let you go."

"You should get to bed, too," he said. "You're working very hard there, I know."

Gincy smiled. "You know me, Ms. Get-'er-done. Good night, Pinky."

"Good night, Brain."

Gincy continued to sit at the kitchen table for a few moments after ending the call with Rick. She needed to think more about the notion of her mother actually needing her; she needed to think more about the notion of her mother actually being glad that her daughter, the prickly, discontented Gincy Gannon, who had rejected a perfectly good life in Appleville for the temptations of the Big City, was there to take care of her, at least for the moment.

And she realized as she sat there that she felt kind of good about it, not of course about her mother being in a state of distress, but about her mother *wanting* her there at Number Nineteen. If indeed Rick was right. After all, everyone needed to be needed, even by a mother who had never shown her daughter much affection or understanding, certainly not once she was past the age of twelve and no longer entirely dependent on her mother for her every thought and opinion. Maybe, Gincy thought now, just maybe Ellen's becoming generally dismissive of her daughter had been the only way she could handle Gincy's growing independence, her obvious desire to leave Appleville, her determination to live a life vastly different from the one her mother had chosen.

It was possible, wasn't it? It was possible that Ellen Gannon had felt rejected by her daughter and had protected herself from hurt in the only way she knew how—by withdrawing, by criticizing. But would Gincy ever really know for sure?

With a sigh, Gincy got up from the table, turned off the kitchen lights, and made her way upstairs to her old bedroom. She had a powerful urge to give her own daughter a great big hug. Tamsin always welcomed hugs.

CHAPTER 26

Ellen and Tamsin were watching a movie in the living room, something starring Ryan Gosling, one of Tamsin's crushes of the moment. The sound was up way too loud, as it had been every time her mother watched a show on television that week, but Gincy refrained from asking them to turn the volume down. For all she knew her mother was experiencing difficulties with her hearing. It was something else she would have to ask about. Carefully, without wounding her mother's pride.

Suddenly, Tommy was standing in the doorway to the kitchen.

"You're like a ninja," Gincy said, her hand to her heart. "You just appear out of thin air."

Tommy grinned. "I came in the front door. You just couldn't hear me because of the TV."

"Is Mom having trouble with her hearing?" she asked.

"She didn't say anything to me." Tommy went over to the fridge, opened it, and began to rummage around. Her father, too, had been one for rummaging. It had driven his wife nuts, Gincy remembered.

Ellen: "Decide what you want before you open the door! You're wasting electricity!"

Ed: "How can I know what's in there if the door is closed?"

Her father had had a point, Gincy thought. She opened one of the drawers under the counter to the left of the sink and began to empty the contents onto the counter. Today one of her chores was drawer tidying; it was amazing what rubbish she had found already, including handfuls of twist ties that had lost most of their plastic covering; three cherry pitters, all broken; and one metal skewer with the word PIG etched into the round end. She had never known either parent to have the need for a metal skewer, ever, not even when the old grill was wheeled out each summer. Ellen and Ed Gannon had cooked hot dogs and hamburgers on the grill, nothing as exotic as kebabs.

And cherries? She had never seen a cherry pass the door of Number Nineteen. Fruit for the Gannons had meant apples, bananas, orange juice, and the occasional grapefruit. Small grapefruit, not medium or large, and always yellow, never pink.

"What's this?" she said, pulling out a bundle of brochures. The brochures, some yellowed with age, were bound in a rubber band, which promptly fell apart as she tried to remove it.

Tommy, still at the fridge, looked over his shoulder. "Those are Mom's," he said. "She's always wanted to go on a cruise to someplace with palm trees and drinks with umbrellas and pieces of fruit stuck in them. She never went. Well, you know that. I guess Dad couldn't afford it."

Gincy stared down at the brochures in disbelief. She had never had any idea her mother wanted to go *anywhere*, let alone on a cruise! As far as she knew, her parents had never gone on vacation other than to a lake on which a distant cousin had a pathetic little cabin with a pathetic little rowboat, and that had been ages ago, before the cousin accidentally set fire to the cabin with his cigarette and it had burned down. For all she knew the rowboat burned, too.

What else about Mom do I not know, Gincy wondered. *Is she a member of the Order of the Eastern Star, a certified pilot, maybe an award-winning chess player?*

Briefly, looking down at the bundle of brochures advertising exotic getaways, the idea of sending her mother on a cruise occurred to her. Why not? She and Rick could probably afford a modest package that included airfare. But was Ellen healthy enough to travel alone? Would she want to? The idea faded away as quickly as it had come.

Tommy closed the fridge without having taken anything out of it and leaned against the counter a few feet from where Gincy was working.

"Mom took good care of Dad," he said.

"What brought that on?" Gincy asked her brother.

"Just thinking. I wish I was as lucky as Dad was. Maybe if I had someone like Mom for a wife I wouldn't . . ."

"You wouldn't what, Tommy?" Gincy asked gently.

"Nothing. Anyway, they were good together. Everybody said so."

Gincy wanted to ask about this "everybody," but it occurred to her that Tommy might think she was challenging him and she didn't want that, not now, not when they were finally really communicating for the first time since they were kids.

"You know," Tommy said then, after glancing toward the door as if to be certain they were alone, "back like seven or eight years ago I signed up for a class at the community college in Brickton."

Gincy was stunned. Tommy barely got out of high school! He had always hated school, right from the beginning, and each year the teachers were glad to see him go.

"You did?" she said. "I never knew that. What sort of a class?"

"Computers."

"Good for you," she said. "Did you enjoy it?"

Tommy picked up a stray jar lid Gincy had found in one of the drawers and began to turn it around and around in his hand. "Not really," he said. "I couldn't keep up. I mean, they had a computer lab where you could practice between classes but . . ."

"Did Mom and Dad know?" Gincy asked.

Tommy glanced again toward the kitchen door. The sound of the television seemed to assure him that his mother was still in the living room. "Nah," he said. "I figured I'd only tell them if I got a good grade or something. I didn't want them to be disappointed."

"Tommy," Gincy said. "Did you finish the class?"

Tommy laughed, and the laugh was bitter. "What do you think?"

"I'm sorry." Gincy, rarely if ever at a loss for words, simply didn't know what else to say.

Tommy shook his head and put the stray lid back on the counter. "Doesn't matter. Do you think Tamsin will be around this afternoon?"

"I suppose. Why don't you ask her?"

Tommy nodded and left the kitchen for the living room.

Gincy felt shaken up by what Tommy had told her—and more so by the fact that he had shared his failure with her in the first place. Her brother had never confided in her about his personal life before this visit home, ever, but maybe that had been her fault. Maybe he had never felt he could trust her not to laugh at him or dismiss his concerns.

"Above all, be kind," Gincy whispered into the empty room.

They certainly *were* words to live by.

CHAPTER 27

Gincy and Ellen spent a good deal of the afternoon running errands. Persuading her mother to accompany her had been oddly easy, and Gincy took that as another sign that her mother was on the road to recovery.

First they dropped off a pair of curtains at the dry cleaners, but only after some verbal tussling. Ellen had insisted that the curtains could be washed by hand in the tiny bathroom tub, and Gincy had strongly vetoed the idea. "Do you know how heavy these will be soaking wet? You'll never be able to handle them, and I'm certainly not going to throw my back out!"

After the dry cleaners they stopped at Harriman's, where Ellen was greeted no fewer than four times, and by name at that, on their way up and down the aisles.

"You're popular, Mom," Gincy said, when one man had gone off after tipping his tweed cap and wishing Ellen the season's greetings. She felt some surprise at this popularity, given her mother's lack of close friends.

"I've lived here a long time," her mother replied. "That's all."

After leaving the grocery store they stopped at a stand

along the road leading out of town. Two teenage boys bundled to the teeth in fleece and wearing goofy knit caps were selling Christmas wreaths. "Our mom makes them," the taller one said when Gincy asked where the wreaths had come from. "She's, like, obsessed," the other boy added. "Our dad said she had to sell some 'cause there's no more room in the house."

"You pick one, Mom," Gincy suggested. "After all, it's for your front door."

"But the cost . . ."

"My gift. Just pick the one you like best."

Ellen chose a wreath of pine boughs heavily decorated with red berries, blue ribbons, and little green bells. There were heavy doses of silver and purple glitter sprinkled over the ribbons.

"It's very—festive," Gincy noted.

Ellen nodded. "It's the nicest wreath by far."

When they got back to the house on Crescent Road, Ellen went to her room for a much needed nap and Gincy went to the basement to fold laundry. The outing had actually been pleasant, she thought, as she stacked clean bath towels and sheets and put aside her mother's blouses for ironing. They had talked about nothing much, certainly nothing to cause either of them distress. Her mother had filled her in on the Appleville gossip, although given her mother's relative social isolation, Gincy couldn't be sure how much of the gossip was up to date. Micky Sullivan might have gotten another job by now, after having been sacked for petty theft at his old job at the hardware store Ed Gannon had once managed. Clarice Huston might have ended her not-so-secret affair with the married pastor at the Baptist Church. And Dr. Hayes might by now have been able to afford to start construction on the new luxury house his wife had been clamoring for.

"That woman," Ellen Gannon had pronounced, "is downright spoiled rotten." Small-town gossip. It was one of the many reasons Gincy was glad to be living in Boston, where a certain degree of anonymity was still possible.

And though she was dying to know more about her mother's secret passion for palm trees and pristine beaches, Gincy had refrained from mentioning the cruise brochures. If her mother had wanted her to know about her interest in ocean travel, wouldn't she have told her before now? She had already pried into her mother's personal life by opening the Bible and, at least in her mother's opinion, by looking through her financial papers.

It was just the three women at dinner that evening. Tommy, after having taken Tamsin to a trolley museum that afternoon, had gone to meet a buddy. Gincy hoped they weren't meeting at a bar, but there was a good chance that they were. Bars were fine in and of themselves; Gincy had spent her fair share of time on a barstool, drinking a beer, munching on French fries or mixed nuts, and pretending to be interested in whatever ball game was on the television over the bartender's head. It was just that Tommy wasn't known for his ability to "drink responsibly." Well, Gincy thought now, maybe that's changed. Tommy had told her that he now liked to work, when for years he had regarded a job as something akin to torture. Maybe these days he had the sense to stop after two or three beers.

"I didn't have any money with me, so Tommy paid our entrance fees," Tamsin told them. "I felt bad. I mean, I didn't know where we were going. If I had, I would have brought some money. It was eight dollars for each of us, and that's because it's off-season. It's ten dollars usually."

"I wonder what made him choose the trolley museum. Had he ever been there before?" Gincy asked.

Tamsin nodded. "Oh, yeah. He said it's his favorite place ever. But he's not an actual member. Maybe it's too expensive to be one."

But ten-dollar entrance fees added up, Gincy thought. Tommy's understanding of economics had never been strong.

"Your grandfather and I went to the trolley museum once," Ellen said. "It was a long time ago. We took Tommy. You didn't want to go with us, Virginia. I don't remember why."

Probably, Gincy thought, *because I was being full of myself and didn't want to be seen with my embarrassing family.*

"Did you have fun?" Gincy asked her daughter.

"I had a great time," Tamsin said. "They've got hundreds of streetcars and trolleys, some dating back to the 1880s. Isn't that amazing? And they've got all these special programs, like one where a real motorman teaches you how to drive a trolley. Tommy said he wants to do that someday. Not be a professional motorman; he just wants to sign up for the program. And you can have a birthday party there, and in October you can ride one of the trolleys out to a pumpkin patch. I'd love to do that."

As her daughter spoke enthusiastically about the T-shirt she would have bought Tommy at the museum shop if she had had any money with her, and what she had learned about the difference between urban and suburban trolleys, Gincy thought back to the conversation she had had with her brother that morning. She thought about how all these years after the ill-fated computer class he still felt the sting of failure. She felt her heart break all over again.

And another thought occurred to Gincy then, as they ate their dinner of cheese ravioli and salad. She had always been critical of her mother's coddling Tommy, of her not pushing him to be better, more productive, to be even a little bit ambitious. She had always thought of her mother, and to a lesser extent of her father, as an enabler. But maybe Ellen had been right all along. Maybe from the start she had known her son's limitations and had accepted him for who he was. Maybe she had known, in the way only a parent could know, that pushing him would only lead to disaster. Maybe her father had known this, too, and had simply loved his son without condition.

The way Gincy loved her own children.

Above all, Gincy thought, her parents had been kind to Tommy.

"How long will you be staying, Virginia?" Ellen asked, when Tamsin had finally finished her report of the afternoon.

"A few more days if that's okay," she said, wondering if her mother had forgotten she had already asked that question.

Ellen's eyes widened. "Of course it's okay. Do you think I would throw my own daughter and granddaughter out of my home?"

Tamsin tried unsuccessfully to hide a grin.

"In fact," Ellen went on, "you could stay through Christmas, if you like."

Gincy hoped that her immediate reaction to this suggestion didn't show on her face. She didn't really *want* to spend Christmas Day at Number Nineteen. She wanted to be home with her husband in their comfortable home, surrounded by the things they had collected together over the years, the paintings, the knickknacks, the books. She wanted to sit under her own real Christmas tree. If that was being childish or selfish, well, that's the way she felt. "Thanks, Mom," she said. "It might depend on work, but I'll let you know as soon as possible."

Ellen nodded. "You decide what's best. And I meant to

tell you, Virginia, I started that new mystery you brought me. When I woke from my nap this afternoon."

"And?"

"It's really very good. It's not too bloody, and there's no bad language. And there are recipes in the back."

"I'm glad you're enjoying the book, Mom," she said, though she dreaded the idea of her mother attempting to make crepes. Regular old pancakes made from a mix were almost beyond her. Ellen never seemed to serve a pancake without a big, fat lump of uncooked dough at its center.

"Do you know if there's a second book in the series already out?" Ellen asked.

"I'll find out for you," Gincy promised. "I'll check the publisher's website."

"That would be nice of you, Virginia."

Well, Gincy thought, that was as close to a "thank you" as she was going to get, but she would take it and be grateful.

"Mom?" Tamsin said. "Do you think we could get Uncle Tommy a membership to the trolley museum for Christmas? I know he'd really like that. You get a free hat with membership. It's a real old-fashioned train engineer's hat. You know the kind."

Gincy smiled. "I don't see why not." And maybe, she thought, the next time she paid a visit to Appleville, she would go to the museum with her brother. And she would not be embarrassed by her family.

CHAPTER 28

"We got more snow," Rick told Gincy when she called him later that evening. "Another two inches."

"Still nothing here," Gincy reported, "though it certainly feels like we're in for some bad weather. It's awfully cold and damp. Which reminds me, I've got to hire someone to shovel for Mom when the snow does hit, which of course it will."

"Winter in New England. What would it be without cars skidding into ditches, frozen water pipes, and a run on emergency generators?"

"Nicer," she said. "Hey, of speaking of the hazards of cold weather, guess what I found today?"

"What?"

"A stack of brochures for cruises to destinations warm and sunny. They're Mom's. Tommy told me."

"Really?" Rick said. "I've never heard your mother mention an interest in going on a cruise."

"Me neither! Imagine, Rick. My mother won't come to Boston because of the strolling rats but she's willing to set sail on a ship with a serious pituitary problem!"

"Your point is what?"

"My point is that ships are notorious for being infested with rats!"

Rick laughed. "Old wooden ships, Gincy. Today's cruise ships are held to a higher standard of cleanliness. Well, okay, maybe they're not but . . ."

"I'm just so surprised, that's all," Gincy said. "My mother—plain, sour-tempered Ellen Gannon—on a cruise. Forced joviality! Dressing up, if people dress up on cruises these days. Sipping cocktails. Watching a magic show. Playing shuffleboard. Isn't that what people do on cruises, play shuffleboard? I just can't picture it. I wonder how Dad felt about taking a cruise. Maybe he told her they didn't have enough money just so he wouldn't have to go."

"Gincy, your father would never have done something so sneaky."

"I know, I know," she said. Then she told Rick about Tommy and the computer class. "I'm still so surprised that he shared that bit of information with me," she said. "I didn't know what to say other than I'm sorry, but I felt awful."

"Poor guy," Rick said. "And not wanting his parents to know. . . ."

"It could break your heart. You know, Rick, I've been so lucky. Being smart, I mean. My brain got me to where I am in life, and yet I've always taken it for granted. I've always been so cavalier about it. My brain and my drive. But I didn't do anything to get this brain and this drive. It's just what I was born with. It's just who I am. How unfair, really. I got so much and Tommy got so little. Life has always been so much more of a struggle for him than it's been for me."

"Life is unfair, Gincy," Rick said gently. "That's just the way it is. But don't forget, it has its good points. Try not to let what's going on in that house totally drag you down."

Gincy laughed. "Christmas cheer and all that? Well, I guess I should sign off. I've been so tired since I've been back home. I mean, to what used to be home. I constantly feel on the verge of a yawn."

"This is probably the longest time you've spent under that roof since you left New Hampshire after high school. Didn't you tell me you spent most of every holiday in the dorms?"

Gincy thought about that for a moment. "You know what?" she said. "You're right. In the dorms or on a friend's sagging couch in some disgusting little apartment in Allston. Being here is a shock to my system."

"Then go to bed," Rick advised. "Sleep is always a good thing."

They said their good-byes. Gincy turned off the lights in the kitchen and made her way upstairs to her old bedroom with the paint peeling off the ceiling and the comfortless mattress.

There were reasons she had stayed away from Appleville, she thought now, and they were good reasons. But maybe those reasons didn't apply anymore, not at this point in her life, not all the time. Maybe going back to where you had come from once in a while wasn't such a bad thing after all, even if it was exhausting and at times disorienting.

It was only when she had tiptoed around her sleeping daughter and was in her bed with the lights turned off that she realized she hadn't told Rick about her mother's offer for her and Tamsin to stay through Christmas Day. Rick would understand if his wife and daughter were compelled to spend the holiday in New Hampshire, and at least he would still get to celebrate the day with Justin.

But still. Gincy really wanted to go home.

CHAPTER 29

At nine the next morning the doorbell rang.

"Who can that be?" Gincy asked. Tamsin, in the kitchen with her mother, shrugged. "No one's come to the house since we've been here but the mailman. It's probably someone trying to sell something or get Mom to sign a petition she won't want to sign. I'll send whomever it is packing."

A moment later she opened the door and exclaimed, "What are you doing here!"

"Hello to you, too, Gincy."

"I didn't ask you to come," Gincy blurted. "I mean, hi."

Clare Wellman Livingston was wearing a well-cut, dusty pink wool coat and a white wool beret. Her small, pale blue leather cross-body bag was from Coach. Clare always carried a Coach bag. Her shoulder-length blond hair was held back in a simple, low ponytail. "It's freezing out here," she said. "Can I come in?"

"Of course. Sorry."

Gincy stepped back, and Clare stepped into the small front hall.

"So," Gincy said, "why are you here? Not that I'm not glad to see you but . . ."

"Tamsin called me," Clare explained. "She asked if I could come for a day to help lift your spirits. School's out for the holiday, and Eason and Sam are happy to have father/son time, so I said, sure. And before you ask, we both agreed not to tell you that I was coming, because you would have put up such a fuss."

Just like Mom would have put up a fuss if she had known that I was coming to visit, Gincy thought. What had Tamsin said the other day? That Gincy and her mother were alike in never asking for help when they needed it.

"Mom," Tamsin said, suddenly standing next to her mother, "face it, you need your friends at a time like this. Grandma is a handful. And I can tell you've been worried about Tommy. Hi, Clare. Thanks for coming."

Clare and Tamsin hugged while Gincy looked on, torn between gratitude and annoyance.

"Well, now that you're here . . ." she said. *Oh boy,* she thought, *there I go again, sounding just like Mom!* "Sorry, Clare. It's great to see you. You look wonderful."

"What's going on? Who is this?"

Gincy turned to her mother, who had joined them in the hall. "This is my friend Clare," she explained. "Clare's surprised us with a visit."

"I hope you don't already have plans, Mrs. Gannon," Clare said, after shaking the older woman's hand. "I was hoping we could all spend the day together. It seemed so silly that we'd never met, and it is the holiday season, so . . ."

Ellen was beaming. Gincy had never seen her mother beam before and was momentarily worried that her blood pressure had risen dangerously.

"That would be lovely," Ellen said. "But you must allow me to change. I won't be a moment."

Tamsin grinned at her mother as Ellen hurried off.

"I can't promise you're going to enjoy yourself," Gincy warned her friend.

"That's not the point of the visit," Clare said. "If I do enjoy myself in the process of taking some of the pressure off you, that's lovely. But it's not what I'm expecting."

"All right, but don't say I didn't warn you."

Clare laughed. "Good old Gincy, Miss Doom and Gloom!"

Ellen returned about five minutes later in a dress Gincy had never seen. Her hair was impeccably done, and she had even put on powder and a bit of lipstick. Ed Gannon would have said that his wife looked spiffy.

"Grandma," Tamsin said. "That's such a pretty dress. I love the shade of blue."

"Thank you, Tamsin," Ellen said. "I only wear it on special occasions."

And it wasn't a special occasion when her daughter came home to visit after an absence of six months? Well, her mother in a nice dress trumped her mother in a badly buttoned cardigan, no matter the reason.

"We can take my car if you like," Clare said when everyone had gotten into coats, hats, mittens and scarves. "It's a monster. There's plenty of room for us all. Eason and I ski," she told Mrs. Gannon, "and he's also a snowboarder, and we camp year round, so we need a huge car to carry all of our equipment."

"Does Sam ski, too?" Tamsin asked. "Sam is Clare's son, Grandma. He's eight."

Clare laughed. "Like a demon."

"How lovely," Ellen said, turning to Gincy.

What was so lovely about the age of eight or skiing like a demon Gincy couldn't say but she smiled and said, "Isn't it."

They were piling into Clare's massive Chevrolet Suburban when Gincy spotted Tommy driving down the street in the direction of the house. She waved to him, but he didn't return her wave or turn into the drive as she expected him to. Instead, he continued on down Crescent Road and was soon out of sight. That was odd, she thought, experiencing a twinge of concern. She wondered if he could have been intimidated by the presence of a newcomer—Tommy's social skills weren't great; in fact, he could be very shy— or maybe it was the obviously expensive vehicle in his mother's driveway that had changed his mind about stopping.

"Wasn't that Uncle Tommy?" Tamsin asked quietly when she and her mother were seated in the back, Gincy behind Clare and Tamsin behind her grandmother.

"Yes."

"I wonder why he didn't stop."

"He was probably on his way to work," Gincy said.

"Where are we going?" Ellen asked when they were all buckled in.

"Well," Clare said, "I saw a sign outside a lovely little church about a mile away. They're having a Christmas fair today. Is anyone interested?"

Ellen shook her head. "The fair went right out of my mind! That's my church, the Church of the Risen Lord."

"That's the one," Clare said.

"I usually work at the fair, helping to sell the baked goods, but . . ."

Tamsin leaned forward and put her hand on her grandmother's shoulder. "This is an adventure, right, Grandma?"

Ellen smiled. "It's a lovely surprise is what it is."

Gincy frowned. Her own surprise visit hadn't been greeted half as enthusiastically. But Clare had the advantage of not being family. Of course Ellen Gannon would be happier to see Clare on her doorstep than her own daughter. It was just the way things were.

Still, Gincy thought grumpily, did her mother have to be quite so ecstatic?

CHAPTER 30

The Christmas fair was already in full swing when they got to the Church of the Risen Lord. It was being held in a basement room that wasn't much larger than the living room at Number Nineteen. Members of the congregation, mostly older women, Gincy noted, were selling homemade cookies and cakes and jams and jellies and pine wreaths and hand-knit scarves and hats and mittens. One long folding table held several rows of old books, spine side up, the hardcovers priced at a dollar and the paperbacks at fifty cents. At another folding table, young girls wearing the uniform of the Girl Squad, an organization Gincy was unfamiliar with, were selling Christmas stockings.

"We made them," a very tall girl announced proudly when the women stopped by to admire. "We learned to sew this summer."

Ellen Gannon smiled at the girl. "It's a fine skill to have," she said. "I wish my own daughter had taken the time to learn. But she was never interested."

It was true, Gincy thought. In their home back in Boston it was Rick who wielded a needle and thread when a button came loose or a pair of Tamsin's jeans needed to be hemmed. He might be accident prone in general and dangerous around kitchen knives, but for some reason he was a whiz with a needle.

The women moved on to the next table, where what looked like the contents of someone's attic were being sold for pennies. Ellen chatted easily with the woman manning the table, asking questions about the old cigar boxes and assorted glass doorknobs and collection of fabric-covered buttons. Before they went on, the woman reached across the table and took Ellen's hand. "It's so good to see you after all this time," she said. "Have a very merry Christmas."

Gincy would have to have been blind and deaf not to see that every person who spoke with her mother that morning said something to the same effect. "Ellen, how lovely to see you! It's been an age!" She thought, too, of the people who had gone out of their way to greet her mother at the grocery store the other day, and she realized that her suspicion that Ellen had been the one to isolate herself after her husband's death had been confirmed. It was certainly good to know that her mother's neighbors hadn't abandoned her. It was sure to put Tamsin's mind at ease, as well.

"You must meet my very good friends!" Ellen suddenly announced, leading Gincy, Tamsin, and Clare over to a table where two women whom Gincy thought looked vaguely familiar were selling raffle tickets.

"Marilyn, Lizzie," Ellen said, "I'd like you to meet my daughter's good friend, Clare. She's come all the way from Maine to spend the day with us! Isn't that wonderful?"

Marilyn and Lizzie made the appropriate noises of welcome and appreciation, shaking Clare's hand and asking how she found "our little town." Clare told the women that she found it charming and bought five dollars' worth of raffle tickets. Then Ellen drew Tamsin forward and introduced her with equal enthusiasm.

I'm the daughter, Gincy thought, feeling a frown come to her face. *Why didn't she introduce me first?*

And then she almost laughed out loud with the shock of it. She was jealous of the attention her mother was heaping on Clare! And she wondered if her mother felt embarrassed by or disappointed in her in some way. Then again, she wasn't at all sure Ellen Gannon had ever harbored particular expectations of her, so how could she possibly have let her mother down?

Tamsin interrupted these disconcerting thoughts.

"Mom," she whispered. "You're frowning."

"Sorry. Just thinking."

"Why does thinking make people frown?"

"I don't know," Gincy admitted. "I'm sure there's some scientific explanation for it."

Tamsin nodded. "I'll look it up."

"Virginia." It was her mother. "Don't just stand there, come and be introduced."

But I've already been introduced, Gincy realized as she stepped forward. *I met these women at Dad's funeral.* But her mother wasn't acknowledging that earlier meeting. Maybe the memories of those trying days were simply too painful for her to recognize. Gincy held her hand out to one of the women at the raffle table, and then to the other. "Hello," she said. "I'm Gincy."

"Virginia," her mother corrected. "I don't know how that silly nickname came to be."

"I hope," Gincy said, "that the fair is a success for the church."

The woman with the short, steel gray hair smiled. "I'm

sure it will be," she said. "God will provide, He always does."

The other woman, the one in a busy holiday-themed sweater, looked to Ellen. "I hope we'll see you at services on Christmas."

Ellen Gannon gave a brief smile but made no commitment. "Virginia," she said, "we should join the others now."

After sitting down for a snack of homemade gingerbread and cups of weak tea, they were able to tear Ellen away from the fair. Her cheeks were bright, whether from the heat generated by the fairgoers packed into the small basement room or from excitement, Gincy couldn't tell.

"Where to next?" Clare asked, starting the engine of the Suburban.

Ellen replied promptly. "Well," she said, "there's a lovely little shop only a few blocks away. It sells the most interesting things. I hope it's still there. I haven't been since the spring. . . ."

"We'll find out," Clare said. "Just point me in the right direction."

Ellen did, and Clare pulled out of the church's parking lot. The woman who had served them tea waved at them as they passed and Ellen nodded back, somewhat regally, Gincy thought.

"I feel like a celebrity," Ellen said. "Don't they all drive these big fancy cars?"

"It's only a jumped-up truck," Gincy muttered to Tamsin. "It's not the Queen's chariot."

"You're jealous that Grandma likes Clare's car better than yours," Tamsin whispered.

"Look!" Ellen cried. "It *is* still here! It really is my favorite shop! Do you know the owner makes all the doilies she sells by hand? Can you imagine the patience it must take?"

Clare found a parking spot a few doors down the street, and Tamsin helped her grandmother descend from her seat.

Ellen laughed. "You almost need a ladder to get into and out of this car!"

"You never mentioned this shop to me, Mom," Gincy said as they approached the storefront, with a prominent sign announcing it as Bea's Hive. "I would have been happy to take you here."

The display windows were crammed full of rag dolls (handmade, Gincy assumed), elaborate wreaths made of woven strips of patterned fabric, colorful pottery in some odd shapes, and large paperback books on topics such as macramé, beading, and baking. Well, Gincy thought, eyeing one of the strange clay pots, maybe she wouldn't have been happy, exactly, to bring her mother to Bea's Hive, but she would have done it. And the holiday fair. If she had known about the fair, she would have offered to take her mother there, too.

Ellen, walking ahead of Gincy and Clare, looked over her shoulder. "I really do think you'll like this store, Clare," she said. "It's not Virginia's taste, of course."

Clare caught Gincy's eye and winked. Gincy grimaced.

Tamsin pushed open the door to the shop and ushered the other women inside, where they were greeted by the cries of a large orange tabby with an alarmingly fat tail and the overwhelming scent of potpourri.

Ugh, Gincy thought. Cats were fine—she admired their attitude—but she loathed potpourri of any sort. What *was* it anyway? Little shredded bits of—what? And why was it so often an awful shade of pinky-purple? As if to prove this loathing, she loudly sneezed.

"Cover your mouth when you sneeze, Virginia," Ellen Gannon said.

"Yes, Mom."

"And use a tissue."

"Yes, Mom." Gincy felt another sneeze coming on. "I think," she said, "that I'd better wait outside."

CHAPTER 31

"I could never eat in a place like that," Ellen Gannon protested from the passenger seat. "It's far too fancy for the likes of me!"

Gincy restrained an eye roll. After all, her mother was probably right. What was Clare thinking, suggesting they have lunch at the Red Rose in Commons Corner? Pretty much everything in Commons Corner, two towns to the west of Appleville, had been out of the Gannons' reach, from the high-end specialty clothing shops, to the exclusive jewelers, to the even more exclusive golf club. And the Red Rose, the town's most popular restaurant, had an excellent reputation for its fine cuisine–and the prices to go with it.

"Don't worry," Clare said firmly. "I have a friend who's eaten there many times and she assures me it's lovely and not at all pretentious. I promise you'll enjoy it."

I hope this friend is right, Gincy thought. She wasn't so sure it was a good idea to take her mother to a relatively upscale restaurant. Would Mrs. Gannon send the milk back claiming it had turned or make no bones about cramming a fistful of sugar packets into her handbag or in some other way annoy the waitstaff so that the service would be horrid or their food poisoned? *There I go again*, she thought, *being dramatic.* Well, if Clare wanted to be the leader of this adventure, fine, Clare could be responsible for the consequences.

But Gincy's fears proved groundless. First, Clare's friend had been right. The Red Rose was lovely and not at all pretentious, and the prices were not as inflated as Gincy had feared. Second, Ellen Gannon conducted herself perfectly, as if she was used to such semiformal surroundings and a waitstaff highly trained in the art of being polite and pleasing. It was Tamsin, if anyone, who seemed a bit overawed by the soft-spoken waitress and the menu that came clipped to a heavy piece of highly polished wood. After the second time she clanged her water glass with the menu, she slipped the board of wood onto her lap and whispered to her mother to please order for her.

As they ate their entrees, Gincy couldn't help but wonder. Had it been in her mother all along, the desire for nice things and the ability to handle new experiences? Maybe she had been doing her mother a disservice, assuming she was "common" just because she couldn't afford a cruise to a tropical island and lunch at the Red Rose. And when had it ever occurred to her to treat her mother to lunch or dinner at a pretty place like this, instead of to the diners and family-style, all-you-can-eat restaurants Ellen Gannon was used to? Suddenly Gincy felt immensely sorry for all the time she had wasted over the years making negative assumptions about her mother.

"Do you know," Ellen Gannon said, turning to Clare, "that Virginia missed being Appleville's first baby of the new year by only three minutes? She was always a stubborn one."

Tamsin quickly took a drink of her water, and Gincy stabbed at her quiche.

Clare, ignoring Mrs. Gannon's comment, said brightly, "I'm sure, Mrs. Gannon, that you know all about that big story the *Globe* ran a few months back, the one exposing a shocking amount of corruption among the administration in some of the city's public schools."

Ellen frowned. "No," she said. "I don't read that paper. My husband used to bring it home but . . ."

Gincy opened her mouth to say something to the effect of, "Clare, please shut up," but before she could speak, Clare was going on with her tale.

"Well," she said, "Gincy was responsible for a large part of the journalistic investigation exposing the people involved. The story earned her a lot of public attention, as well as an award from the official journalism community."

Ellen turned to her daughter, a look of—was it confusion?—on her face. "You never mentioned an award to me, Virginia," she said.

Gincy shrugged. Public recognition of her accomplishments had always made her feel awkward, even as a kid. But would she have told her father about the award, if it had been given to her when he was still alive? Yes, she thought. She probably would have.

"I didn't think you were interested in my work," she said to her mother.

"Well, of course I'm interested," Ellen replied, her eyes wide. "Why would you ever think otherwise?"

"Mom just doesn't like to toot her own horn," Tamsin said.

"That's true," Clare added with a smile. "You might not think it at first, but she's actually quite humble."

"All right, guys," Gincy said, with an embarrassed smile. "Enough."

When the women had placed their dessert orders, Clare once again steered the conversation to the subject of her friend's vast accomplishments.

"Gincy," she said, "I've been meaning to ask you about that organization you volunteer for, the Voter Education Initiative."

Gincy shrugged. "It's going well."

"It's going more than just well," Tamsin added excitedly. "Mom organized the latest outreach to the immigrant communities, you know, trying to get people ready for citizenship and to convince the ones who are already citizens that they should vote. It was a huge success, and Mom's picture was on the cover of the monthly newsletter and she got a personal note from the governor, thanking her for all her hard work!"

Ellen Gannon turned to her daughter. "I never knew you were interested in such things, Virginia."

You've never asked what interests me, Gincy thought. Then again, she had never volunteered much about herself to her mother. Why? Her much touted humility? Or was there another reason? Relationships were a two-way street. They both had been at fault in not pursuing knowledge of each other. But she said none of this aloud.

"And when another volunteer flakes out," Tamsin was saying, "Mom's the first person they call."

"Her father was a hard worker, too," Ellen said with a conclusive nod. "That's where she gets it from. Reliability. I could always rely on Virginia's father."

Gincy didn't know whether to beg her daughter to stop talking, to thank her mother for the roundabout compliment, or to crawl under the table. She was prevented from any of these options by the arrival of their waitress with the desserts.

Ellen had ordered a slice of key lime pie. Her choice had

surprised Gincy; she would have sworn that her mother had never even heard of key limes let alone key lime pie. But maybe the idea of key lime pie made Ellen Gannon think of tropical climes and palm trees and cruise ships.

"I wish you could bake like this, Virginia," Ellen said when she was halfway through the dessert. "You never could make a decent piecrust."

What did her mother know about piecrust, Gincy wondered? The few times she had even made a pie she had used a prebaked frozen crust from Harriman's.

"Maybe I'll take a course in pastry at the CIA," Gincy said, unable to keep a trace of perversity out of her tone. "Maybe I'll give up my job in print journalism and become a professional pastry chef."

Ellen frowned. "There's no need to go to extremes, Virginia."

Well, Gincy thought, her mother was in no danger of developing a sense of humor.

Clare excused herself to pay a visit to the ladies' room. As soon as she was out of sight, Ellen leaned across the table toward her daughter. "She's so pretty and charming! She seems like such a wholesome person." And then she sighed. "If only you had had a real wedding in Appleville, I could have met her long ago."

"I really like that pair of mittens you got at the fair, Grandma," Tamsin said brightly. "They're a nice color green. Who are they for?"

"I thought I would give them to Tommy," Ellen said. "He's always losing his gloves and mittens. He must have gone through four or five pair last winter."

Tamsin smiled. "Too bad he's not a little kid anymore. Then you could clip his mittens to the sleeves of his jacket."

The image almost made Gincy smile. Almost. Where

would her brother be without their mother? She had never heard her mother say a critical or judgmental thing about her son—the one family member who, some might say "deserved" criticism or judgment. Her mother was kind to her son, if not always kind or pleasant to her daughter, but really, Gincy thought, why do I need kindness from her if it's something she simply can't give? What had Danielle said? Her mother gave what she had to give. It was all anyone could do, really.

Clare returned and took her seat at the table.

"Maybe you can help me with something, Clare," Gincy said. "I'm trying to get Mom to see her doctor."

"But I'm not sick," Ellen protested. "It's a waste of time and money, I've told Virginia that."

"Mom, you've lost weight. Maybe it means nothing but . . ."

"I think Gincy is right, Mrs. Gannon," Clare said. "It will put everyone's mind to rest if the doctor gives you a clean bill of health."

Ellen nodded. "Well, Clare, if you really think that I should see my doctor, I will."

"Good," Gincy said. "I'll make an appointment first thing tomorrow."

"I'm perfectly capable of making the appointment, Virginia."

Seek peace and pursue it, Gincy thought. At least her mother had agreed to the visit. "Okay, Mom," she said. "If you'd rather call."

CHAPTER 32

At the end of the afternoon Clare brought the family back to Number Nineteen Crescent Road. She came inside with them to say her good-byes.

"It was so good to meet you, Mrs. Gannon," she said, giving the older woman a gentle hug. "Thank you for allowing me to spend the day with you."

She always knows exactly the right thing to say, Gincy thought. If only Clare would give lessons in being politic, she would be the first to sign up.

Ellen laughed. "I'm suddenly so tired! I can't remember when I've had such a nice day. Thank you, Clare. You drive safely now. Virginia, I'm going to lie down for a while before dinner."

Mrs. Gannon went off to her room.

"How can I thank you for what you did for us today?" Gincy said when her mother had gone. "You know, I think my mother probably wishes you were her daughter instead of me."

"Mom!" Tamsin cried. "That's not true!"

Clare laughed. "I was just a change for her. And maybe I was able to give her a glimpse into her daughter's professional world, a world I'm guessing she knows very little about and probably assumes would intimidate her if she did."

"Whatever the case, it was like being with a different woman today, almost a stranger," Gincy said. "Except for the criticizing."

"We all have trouble really seeing those people closest to us," Clare said. "My presence helped you to get a bit of a new perspective on your mom, and maybe helped her get a bit of a new perspective on you, that's all. And honestly? I don't think your mother is half aware that she's criticizing you. I think it's just the habit of a lifetime. Just how she talks to you. Automatic behavior."

"I think Clare is right, Mom," Tamsin said. "I think it's, like, unconscious."

Gincy frowned. "It's still annoying."

"I know," Clare said sympathetically.

"I mean, she's so perverse with me, so contradictory. If I said that the sweater I'm wearing is blue, which as you can see it is, she'd say, 'Nonsense, Virginia, that sweater is green.' "

Clare laughed again. "Sorry, but it is funny in its way."

Gincy thought about that for a moment. And then she said, "You know what? It is sort of funny."

The three said their good-byes and Clare prepared to head north. "Visit me," she called as she pulled away in her massive vehicle. "Remember, life in Maine is the way life should be!"

Except for the ice-fishing, Gincy thought. The Mainers could keep that all to themselves. And the moose. They could keep those, too.

"I think Grandma really enjoyed herself today," Tamsin said when she and her mother had gone to the kitchen to prepare for dinner.

"Me too. You were right to invite Clare, Tamsin. I guess we needed an infusion from the outside world. We needed a breath of fresh air. Family can be so claustrophobic."

"I think it's the ideas you have of your family that makes being with them feel claustrophobic," Tamsin said. "I mean, if you could magically meet your father or sister or whoever for the first time with no memories of them, you'd be meeting a totally different person from the one you knew. Or something like that."

Gincy nodded. "You're right. The bad part of familial relationships aren't really the people themselves but the accumulated resentments and prejudices and imagined slights and distorted memories."

"Maybe Danielle can come spend a day with us, too," Tamsin suggested. "Maybe she could bring her girls! I haven't seen them in, like, forever."

"Well," Gincy said, "I think we'll be all right from this point on. But you never know."

"Grandma ate a huge lunch. Do you think she'll be able to eat dinner?"

Gincy grinned. "I think she'll manage to choke down a morsel or two!"

"And I'm setting the table for four, just in case Uncle Tommy decides to show up."

"Thanks," Gincy said. "Thank you."

"Mom? We'd already met those women from the fair, didn't we? Marilyn and Lizzie. Back at Grandpa's funeral."

"Yes," Gincy said. "We did."

Tamsin frowned. "Do you think Grandma just forgot that she'd introduced us before?"

"No, Tamsin," Gincy said. "I think that she remembers it all too well."

CHAPTER 33

"She was in fine form today, my mother was. She was literally fawning over Clare!"

Rick laughed. "People do tend to have that reaction to Clare. Maybe it's the blond hair and the perfectly coordinated outfits. More likely it's her kindness."

"Yeah, well," Gincy said, "I have to admit it annoyed me at first—a lot, actually—but then I got over it. And it's hard to be mad at Clare. All she was doing was being her charming self."

"It was seriously nice of her to visit. You've got two really good friends in Clare and Danielle."

"Don't I know it! And one very crafty daughter. Imagine her calling Clare behind my back."

"I'd say Tamsin is resourceful," Rick said, "rather than crafty."

"And Mom even paid me a compliment, sort of. She said I got my hard work ethic from my father."

"Sounds like a genuine compliment to me," Rick said. "She acknowledged that you're a hard worker. And that's something you take pride in."

"There was one odd thing about the day, though," Gincy went on. "As we were getting into Clare's car, Tommy drove by. I'm pretty sure he was on his way here, to the house, but then he just kept going. And he didn't wave back when I waved to him. I don't know, I can't help but feel he might have been intimidated by the sight of Clare's big expensive car or . . . I don't know. Anyway, I told Tamsin that he probably didn't stop because he was on his way to work."

"Maybe he really was on his way to work," Rick pointed out.

"The convenience store is in the opposite direction."

"Have you called him since then?"

"No, but I will, later. And Mom ate a big dinner, after an even bigger lunch and a snack after breakfast. I don't think we have to worry about the weight issue anymore, at least for the moment. Though Clare did get her to agree to see her doctor, and that was something I couldn't do."

"Good," Rick said. "That's one big goal accomplished."

"Are you watering the tree?"

"Yes, Gincy," Rick said. "I'm watering the tree."

When Rick had gone off to watch the latest episode of whatever cable series he was currently addicted to—Gincy could hardly keep track of his television obsessions—she tried her brother on his cell, but the call went to voice mail. "Call me," she told him. "Nothing's wrong, but let me hear from you."

Then she remembered that Tommy had—or had once had—a landline. The number would still be in her mother's old address book. With some difficulty she found it—for some reason the number was in the "S" section; for son?—

then she dialed. A recorded message informed her that the number was no longer in service.

Well, she thought. If her mother wasn't worried about Tommy and his erratic appearances, then she shouldn't be worried, either.

But she was.

CHAPTER 34

By a bit of luck, Ellen Gannon's GP was able to see her the next morning. "People often cancel right before a holiday," the receptionist had explained to Gincy, who, in actuality, had been the one to call the office. "I don't think anyone wants to risk hearing bad news about their heart right before they're off to celebrate with calorie and cholesterol-laden meals."

Dr. Walker was about forty. He made Gincy feel old. It always made her feel old when she encountered younger authority figures. Police officers, doctors, lawyers, all barely out of diapers! Well, that was an exaggeration. Still. She didn't like it.

"So how is my mother, Doctor?" Gincy asked when the exam was over and she had been called into the examination room.

"Fit as a fiddle, though a bit too thin and possibly anemic, but the blood tests will tell us for sure. All fairly easy to fix," he said with a smile.

"You see, Mom?" Gincy said. "It was a good thing we came."

Ellen nodded. "Yes, Virginia."

Dr. Walker put his hand on his patient's shoulder. "Mrs. Gannon, I would strongly advise you to listen to your daughter. She only wants what's best for you."

That was true, Gincy thought, looking at her mother sitting now in the visitor's chair, her old pocketbook, the "good" one, held firmly in her lap, her best shoes shined just that morning. She did want what was best for her mother. But she didn't deserve praise for it. What halfway decent daughter didn't want what was best for her mother?

"You know, Dr. Walker," Ellen said, "my daughter has made quite a success of her life. She made a good match, her husband is a very nice man, and she's a real bigwig in Boston. Between you and me, that important newspaper she works for is probably going bankrupt without her there in the office to see that things happen properly."

Gincy cringed at her mother's gross exaggeration of the extent of her professional power. And yet she was touched. No child was ever too old to appreciate a parent's approval. She remembered what her mother had supposedly told Adele Brown, that she didn't want to disturb her daughter because of her big important job in the city. . . .

Over her mother's head, Dr. Walker gave Gincy a conspiratorial smile. "All the more reason, Mrs. Gannon, that you should take your daughter's advice."

They thanked the doctor and made their way back to the waiting area. "Have a seat for a minute, Mom," Gincy said. "I'm going to use the ladies' room."

But Gincy had no need of the ladies' room. Instead, she asked to speak for a moment to the nurse practitioner, a woman much closer to Gincy's age than Dr. Walker. Briefly, she told the woman about her mother's depression. "I do think she's coming out of it," she said, "but I worry she'll have a relapse, possibly once I've gone back home to Boston."

"Any chance she could go to stay with you for a bit?" the nurse practitioner asked.

"Doubtful. I mean, my husband and I would be fine with it, but my mother is fairly terrified of the city."

"Well, at least you can continue to keep a close eye on her while you're here," the nurse advised. "If you see any deterioration, bring her in. Depression is certainly not uncommon after the loss of a spouse, especially at the holidays. We can try a mild antidepressant."

Gincy thanked the nurse and headed back to the reception area. She highly doubted her mother would take an antidepressant willingly, but it was good to know there were options besides seeing a therapist, something she knew for sure her mother would never, ever do. Cities and therapists were firmly on Ellen Gannon's list of things to be avoided at all costs.

"What took you so long?" Ellen demanded when Gincy rejoined her. "I'm getting hungry. You heard what the doctor said. He says I have to eat more."

Gincy smiled. "How about a hamburger for lunch, Mom? The doctor said you need more protein in your diet."

"If you say so, Virginia."

"I do, Mom," Gincy said. "I say so."

CHAPTER 35

After lunch, Ellen went to her room for a nap. Tamsin, after helping her mother clean up the kitchen, announced that she was going to walk downtown.

"I noticed this new store on Main Street while we were driving around yesterday," she said. "They've got those nautical-style rope bracelets I like. I want to see how much they cost."

"They're probably cheaper here than in Boston," Gincy noted. "Most everything is."

When Tamsin had gone off, Gincy called Tommy's cell, but again the call went to voice mail. "Call me, Tommy," she told him. Where the heck was he, she thought. Why couldn't he at least return a call? It wasn't lost on her that only weeks ago Tommy's silence would have annoyed her. Now what she felt was concern. Was he sick? In trouble?

Gincy sighed. So much in one's life could change in a matter of days, even moments. Even long-held estimations of a person could be thoroughly wiped away in the proverbial heartbeat and you could suddenly start to see him as he really was. What was the old expression, probably from the

Bible or Shakespeare? Most great expressions were. The scales were falling from her eyes.

Gincy sighed. Suddenly, the idea of a nap, or at least of a rest, seemed a good one. She went up to her old room and lay down on the ancient mattress. And not surprisingly she found herself thinking back to that pivotal summer of her life, the summer she met Rick and Clare and Danielle. In fact, she dated the start of her adult life to that summer. Clare and Danielle had become her first genuine friends, though initially she was absolutely sure they would never be close. And she hadn't been at all interested in getting seriously involved with a man, let alone a widower with a small child!

So much had changed for her that summer. She had learned so much. She had finally, at the age of twenty-nine, grown up.

She remembered now the call she had gotten from her father one hot and humid night. She had immediately assumed that he had bad news to tell her. Her father was *never* the one to call. "Who's dead?" she had demanded.

But Ed Gannon had contacted his daughter for quite a different reason. After an unexpected visit to his sister, Tommy had gone home to Appleville to report that Gincy was seeing a creepy old guy. Ed Gannon was concerned. What exactly had her father said to her? Yes, that she had always had good sense but that as her father he felt he should offer a warning about men. She had assured him that Rick was neither creepy nor old and had thanked him for his concern. He had told her to call him if she needed anything.

It had been a turning point for Gincy, that simple conversation with her father. She had realized that until that moment she hadn't given him much credit for anything other than being a hard and conscientious worker. She certainly had never given him credit for caring enough to reach out to her when he thought she might be in trouble.

She had made a separate peace with her father after that. Then why not with her mother? What had been holding her back besides stubbornness? And it wasn't her mother's responsibility to make the effort to connect. It was Gincy's duty to reach out. She believed that. For one, she had seen a lot more of the world than her mother had. She was more emotionally equipped to take a risk.

As if to prove this to herself, she set her mind to recall times when her mother had indeed been a good and loving parent. Surprisingly, as they had done the other day when she had thought about the picnics and the bake sales, the memories of those early days came easily. For one, there was the year her mother had made her a fantastic Halloween costume in a matter of hours.

Gincy had been invited to a party given by a girl at school, but for some reason she couldn't now recall (something silly, no doubt; even as a kid she had been quick to take offense) she had gotten mad at the girl and announced that she wouldn't be coming to her "stupid boring party." Then, for another reason she couldn't now recall (probably something equally as silly), she had changed her mind.

"I need a costume for Margaret's party tomorrow afternoon," she had told her mother.

"Use the money you've been saving from babysitting and buy a costume at the variety store," her mother had replied, not raising her eyes from the local newspaper she was reading.

"But I don't have enough money for a good costume! I'll look totally stupid!"

And then she had stamped her foot. This had gotten her

mother's full attention, and after some scolding about breaking promises and paying the consequences, Mrs. Gannon had gone off to her sewing machine. By the morning she had produced an accurate replica of Wonder Woman's costume, albeit with a more demure neckline. Gincy doubted that *she* would have been so accommodating to a whiny, obnoxious eleven-year-old, and certainly not to one who had gone so far as to stamp her foot.

Then there was the time in her sophomore year of high school—and this was embarrassing to recall, even all these years later—when she had fallen under the spell of a girl named Kathy O'Connell. The kid was bad news all around, but Gincy, chafing under the constraints of life in Appleville, had found in this criminal in the making a hero, rather, an antihero who was living out some pathetic rebel fantasy, smoking filterless cigarettes, scowling a lot, and generally causing mayhem. She still remembered with incredible clarity the day Kathy told her she was planning to break into the Kmart out on the highway and wanted her help, and the feeling of almost sexual thrill that had overcome her. *This* was what life was about. *This* was excitement!

In the end Gincy had backed out of the scheme, stoically enduring Kathy's nasty verbal abuse. Well, Kathy had gone ahead with the robbery and had gotten caught red-handed, so she had probably endured her own share of verbal abuse, though she probably had not done so stoically.

Now, all these years later, lying on her old narrow bed, something came to Gincy, something she remembered having heard her mother say that had tipped the scales in favor of sanity and maturity, something that had given her the courage to say no to Kathy.

Her parents had been watching the local evening news,

and she had been doing her homework at the kitchen table. She had gone into the living room at one point to retrieve a notebook she had left there. She remembered her father shaking his head and saying, "How can a person stand to look at himself in the mirror after committing a crime like that?" There was nothing unusual in his comment, nothing to grab her attention. She was on the way out of the living room, notebook in her hand, when her mother had said, "Forget about looking at himself in the mirror. Everyone lets himself off the hook in the end. Everyone learns to live with himself. The real question is, how can he ever hold his head up in public? It's what other people think of us that really matters. How can he ever bear to walk down a street knowing that his neighbors know what a stupid, cowardly thing he's done? How can he bear the shame?"

Gincy remembered lying awake on her bed that night, thinking about what her mother had said. Thinking about shame. Thinking about responsibility. Thinking about how important it was not to be ostracized from the very community that had fostered you. Rebellion was all well and good but only if what you were rebelling against was truly awful and personally destructive. Her hometown might not be ideal, and already, at the age of fifteen, Gincy knew she would be leaving it one day, but she didn't need to be leaving it in disgrace. And the very next day she had told Kathy to count her out of her stupid criminal scheme.

So it was Mom who kept me out of juvenile detention, Gincy thought, lying on that same old bed in that same old room. Imagine that. And maybe it was her mother—and her father, when he was alive—who had kept Tommy on the straight and narrow for so long now.

Pretty good accomplishments as far as parenting went, Gincy thought, glancing over at her mother's sewing machine. Really, how much more could you ask for from your mother and father than a good grounding in the difference between right and wrong?

And maybe, on occasion, an awesome Halloween costume and bologna sandwiches in the park.

CHAPTER 36

Once Tamsin had come back to Number Nineteen, wearing her new bracelet—"It only cost fifteen dollars! They're like fifty dollars in Boston!"—Gincy got in her car and drove to Appleville Park. It was as gray and bleak and sad looking as it had been a few days earlier, but for a reason Gincy couldn't name, she felt the need to be there. Maybe it was the happy memories of the splashing fountain or the thought of how lovely the park would look covered in a blanket of snow. She took a seat on the same bench where she had called Danielle and pressed the button for Rick's cell.

"You know what?" she said when Rick answered.

"What?"

"I'm an idiot."

"Now, Gincy," Rick said, "not all of the time."

"Rick! I mean it. I'm an idiot. But I've had a revelation. All these years I've been so unfair to my mother, punishing her because, I don't know, because she's not me. What's so great about me that my mother should want to be my double?"

"A lot is great about you, Gincy," Rick said, "but I hear what you're saying."

"Why haven't I been able to accept her for who she is? Well, there are probably a thousand reasons, but it stops now. I swear I'm going to try seriously hard to stop judging and complaining about her and just—accept."

"It won't be easy, you know," Rick said. "The habits of a lifetime are hard to break, and your mother can be difficult."

"I know," Gincy admitted. "I'll probably fail miserably at first, but I'll keep at it and eventually I'll get it right."

"There's the spirit."

"Do you know what Mom said to the doctor this morning? She's fine, by the way, possibly a bit anemic. She told him I had made a real success of my life. I swear I almost had a heart attack. I certainly never knew my mother to brag about me!"

"You haven't been drugging her food, slipping happy pills into her afternoon tea?"

Gincy laughed. "Would that it were so simple."

"And not that you would ever do such a thing."

"Of course not," Gincy said. "I don't think that I would. Anyway, the problem is that I don't know what to *do*. Do I tell her I'm sorry for being a jerk? Will she even know what I mean? Will she *pretend* not to understand, just to punish me? Should I say nothing and just go ahead with my plan of acceptance? Help me out here, Rick."

"I wish I could, Gincy," her husband said, "but I'm not sure I know the answer to that. What I do know is that you shouldn't expect any big change on your mother's part just because you feel a change of heart or perspective. You'll just be letting yourself in for disappointment. Remember what I said a few minutes ago. She can be difficult."

"And so," Gincy said, "can I."

"Only sometimes. Hey, speaking of difficult, any word from your brother?"

"No, but Mom insists there's nothing to worry about."

"She probably knows best where Tommy's concerned. Try not to get yourself worked up."

"Me? Worked up." Gincy laughed. "Never. Still, I wish he'd come home. I'm trying to change my way of thinking about Tommy, too. Well, I guess you've picked up on that."

"I have," Rick said. "And I think you'll have an easier time of things with your brother than with your mother. But hang in there, Gincy. You've got backup in me and your children and your friends."

"Thanks, Rick. I'd better get back to the house. Are you—"

"Yes, Gincy," Rick said. "I've been watering the tree."

Gincy laughed again. "Good. Because as Dad used to say, you can never be too careful."

CHAPTER 37

Gincy made spaghetti and meatballs for dinner, with a side of broccoli. There was no use in making anything even remotely interesting or gourmet for her mother. (Even at the Red Rose she had ordered the basic dish of chicken potpie, though the key lime pie for dessert had been a surprise.) In truth, that was fine with Gincy, whose culinary tastes had always run to the basic. There were years when she was young and single when she pretty much survived on chips and pizza and beer and soda. Though she wouldn't tell Rick, who did most of the cooking at home and who made it a rule to vary his menus, sometimes she missed those bad old days when she considered nachos a well-balanced meal.

"How did the visit to the doctor go, Grandma?" Tamsin asked when they were settled at the table.

"I'm perfectly fine," Ellen told her. "I told your mother she was worried about nothing."

"But Clare thought it was a good idea, too," Tamsin said, "seeing the doctor."

"Better safe than sorry, as Dad always said."

Ellen nodded. "Your father was a smart man. I've always said that you're a lot like him, Virginia."

Tamsin's eyes widened.

Gincy almost fell out of her chair. She was hardworking and smart. She was reliable. The *Globe* was going bankrupt without her. She had married well. What was next?

"Has anyone seen or heard from Tommy today?" she asked. She hadn't mentioned the defunct landline to her mother but wondered now if she should.

Tamsin shook her head. "I called him a few times on his cell but he never answered."

"Is that typical, Mom?" Gincy asked. "That he doesn't answer his cell phone?"

"As I told you the other day, Virginia, Tommy is his own man. I'm sure he's fine. He's never out of touch for long."

"Yes, but . . . All right," Gincy said. "If you say it's okay."

How hard it must have been, Gincy thought—how hard it still must be for her mother (and once, her father)—to love Tommy and to accept him just the way he was. How hard it must have been not to feel disappointed in their son, but to let love and kindness win out over criticism and unfair expectations.

Above all, be kind to those you love.

"Well," Gincy said, "if he comes by later I can heat up our leftovers for him. I made more than enough for four people."

Ellen smiled at her daughter. "I'm sure he would appreciate that."

"Mom? Do you remember that Wonder Woman costume you made me one Halloween?"

Ellen frowned. "Vaguely, yes. Why?"

"Do you know if it's still around? I thought I'd show it to Tamsin."

"Now, Virginia, I'm sure I threw it out long ago. Why would I have kept such a thing?"

"No reason, Mom. I was just wondering."

"I do recall," Ellen said musingly, "that it was a very good costume."

"It was the best, Mom," Gincy said. "It was the best costume at the party."

CHAPTER 38

"What do you think, Mom? Santa's sleigh facing to the right or to the left?"

Tamsin was crouched at the base of the old, indestructible tree where she was setting up a Christmas tableau on a blanket of cotton snow. The tableau featured a miniature Victorian village, including a bank, post office, tavern, and grammar school, and figurines representing a mother, father, two children, two grandparents, and a dog vaguely resembling a spaniel of some sort.

Earlier that day Tamsin and her mother had gone downtown to gather a few more holiday decorations for Number Nineteen. At Ellen's favorite shop (Gincy holding her glove to her nose the entire time they were there) Tamsin had fallen in love with the Victorian village, and though it was a bit pricey it was awfully charming, and Gincy had agreed they should buy it for her mother.

"I don't think it matters from which direction Santa is coming," Gincy said. "I think people are just happy that he's paying them a visit."

Tamsin laughed. "I suppose you're right."

They had ignored the giant box of lights they had found in the basement, most of which Gincy figured were probably burned out, and bought several boxes of new tiny white lights at the hardware store Ed Gannon used to manage. No one working there now was old enough to have a personal memory of Ed Gannon, and no one recognized Gincy as his daughter. *Everything changes*, Gincy thought, glancing at the key-making machine as they left the old store. *Everything.*

Together she and Tamsin had strung a line of twinklers (that was Tamsin's word for the little lights) around the living room window and another around the windows of the upstairs bedrooms. Once Gincy had nailed to the front door the gaudily decorated wreath her mother had chosen the other day, the house finally looked appropriately festive.

"Now we can decorate the tree," Tamsin said, rising from the floor. "I'll open the boxes."

"You'll get dust all over your clothes," Gincy warned. "I don't know how they got so dusty in the basement. Dad kept things so clean down there."

Tamsin shrugged and unfolded the flaps of the three cardboard boxes lined up on the floor. Gincy watched as her daughter began to lift out the ornaments that had been in the Gannon family for at least fifty years.

Gincy grimaced as Tamsin held up a crocheted . . . thing. It was an unhappy combination of browns and beiges, and around one end was tied a red ribbon. "What is this supposed to be?" Tamsin asked.

"I was never sure," Gincy admitted. "An animal of some sort? A Christmas snake? And I have no idea where it came from."

Tamsin turned the thing over in her hand. "I don't see

any eyes or nose or mouth. Maybe they fell off." Tamsin shrugged, tossed the thing onto the couch, and continued to unpack the boxes. There was no doubt about it, Gincy thought. Most of the ornaments were tacky at best and ugly at worst—cheesy plastic elves in sequin bodysuits; leering, drunken-looking Santas; creepy snowmen made of oversized cotton balls badly glued together, with small black buttons for eyes. What, she wondered, had possessed her mother—or had it been her father?—to choose these things over classic glass ornaments and delicate silvery tinsel? Maybe, she thought, her parents hadn't had the money for nicer ornaments. Maybe they had simply *liked* the poorly constructed snowmen and sparkly elves. And that was fine, too.

"Wait," Gincy said, "what's that?" She reached into the box Tamsin was unpacking. Something had caught her eye. . . .

"What is it, Mom?"

Gincy held out a slightly damaged Styrofoam ball now only partly covered in green glitter. At the top of the ball a small plastic hook protruded.

"Tommy and I made these," she told her daughter "When he was about five and I was about ten. There were at least three or four of them."

Tamsin made a quick search of the box. "That's the only one left, I think," she said.

Gincy gazed at the little ball, and suddenly she was forty years in the past and she and her little brother were sitting at the kitchen table, craft materials spread out before them on a single layer of newspaper. Her mother, she remembered, had left the kitchen for some reason, and not a minute after she had gone one of them—but which one? She couldn't remember!—had poured a handful of glitter from its narrow plastic tube and tossed it into the air.

A full-blown glitter war had ensued, with glue squirting across the table and glitter descending in clouds onto every surface of the kitchen. Gincy smiled. She and Tommy had been punished for making a mess, but boy it had been fun while it lasted. She would ask Tommy if he remembered that day when he next came by.

"Still no word from Tommy?" Gincy asked, after securing the ball to a branch of the tree.

Tamsin shook her head. "He hasn't called me. Maybe he's talked to Grandma."

"Maybe I should go around to his place. See for myself if he's all right."

"Grandma says he always turns up. . . . But maybe you should go, Mom. I could come with you."

"No," Gincy said firmly. "If I go, I'll go alone." The last thing she wanted was for her daughter to witness her uncle in serious distress. Or worse.

And suddenly another old memory struck her, and with force. She must have been around eight, making Tommy about three. They were in a neighbor's yard or maybe at the public playground. For the life of her she couldn't remember either of her parents being around. If they were, it would put the lie to the rest of the memory, which was an image of Tommy falling and hitting his head on the edge of a sandbox. There was blood, what seemed like a lot of it. And then she was lifting her brother into her arms. He was crying and screaming and she, a skinny little kid, was stumbling along under his weight, telling him it would be okay. Taking him home.

What exactly had happened after that, Gincy couldn't recall. She did know that Tommy had been fine. He hadn't needed stitches, and there hadn't even been a scar to memorialize the event. But she remembered the day now, as clearly as if it were yesterday. . . .

"Mom," Tamsin said. "Are you crying?"

Gincy startled and forced her eyes wide. They were a bit wet. "Of course not," she said. "Why would I be crying?"

Tamsin shrugged. "This fire engine ornament," she said, holding up a battered bit of tin. "Was it Tommy's?"

Gincy laughed. "It was mine. For a time when I was little, I wanted to be a fireman. There were no women firefighters back then—okay, I'm old—but I didn't see why that should stop me."

"Good for you, Mom!" Tamsin cried. "A woman before your time! What did Tommy want to be?"

Gincy thought hard. "I know," she said after a moment. "When he was very little, maybe three or four, he said that he wanted to be a rock. How odd that memory should come to me now, after all these years. And how odd that he should have wanted to be a rock. Why a rock, I wonder."

"Maybe he meant something else but he didn't have the word for it," Tamsin suggested. "Little kids always mess up words."

"You mean he really wanted to be a sock? Or a clock?"

"Ha, ha. Maybe he heard someone saying that someone else was dependable like a rock and he thought, 'That's what I want to be.'"

"We'll never know," Gincy said, "unless we ask him, but I doubt he'd remember that far back."

"You know, Mom, when Uncle Tommy and I went to the trolley museum the other day, he told me he really misses Grandpa. He said they used to watch ball games together all the time, football in the fall and baseball in the spring."

"Did they?" Gincy said with a smile. "I didn't know. Well, I'm glad Tommy was able to share that with you. I don't know much about his friends, such as they are. I suspect they're not really a support system, just drinking buddies."

But maybe, Gincy thought, drinking buddies were enough for Tommy, as long as he had his family. As long as his family didn't let him down, especially now that Ed Gannon was gone. She made a mental note to ask Rick about giving Tommy money enough to either repair his truck or buy a decent used one. And when they had finished decorating Number Nineteen for the holiday, she would get in her car and drive to Tommy's apartment. No matter what she found there, knowing was better than not knowing.

"You're not hanging that candy cane properly, Virginia. Here, let me do it."

Gincy turned to see her mother standing at the entrance to the living room. Since when, she thought, was there a right or a wrong way to hang a candy cane? Only one end had a hook! She remembered what Clare had said the other day—there *was* something funny about her mother's habit of contradiction and criticism. Gincy handed the candy cane to her mother. "Here you go, Mom," she said.

"Oh," Ellen said, then, giving the candy cane a final small adjustment on its branch, "I just spoke to your brother. He's fine, like I told you, Virginia. His boss at the convenience store gave him more hours this week and he's been busy."

"I'm so glad he's okay!" Tamsin cried.

Gincy, too, felt enormous relief, but she still wished her brother had called her back. But why should he have, she thought. She had never shown any real interest in him since the very earliest days; she had never expressed any real concern after they were small children. How would he possibly know that she cared about his welfare? A few calls to his cell phone couldn't make up for years of neglect.

"That's a lovely village!" Ellen said, pointing down at Tamsin's arrangement on the white cotton snow. "Is that for me? Where did it come from?"

"We got it at your favorite store, Grandma, the one you took us to with Clare. Bea's Hive."

"Well . . ." Ellen cleared her throat. "Thank you, Tamsin."

Gincy was reaching for one of the awful little elves to hang next to a candy cane when she became aware that her mother had turned her attention away from the Victorian village under the tree and was eying her critically, from head to foot and back again.

"Mom," she said. "What are you looking at?"

"You don't look as wrinkled and messy as you used to, Virginia."

Tamsin tried but failed to hide her smile.

"Thanks, Mom," Gincy said. And to be fair, she thought, she *had* used to dress like a slob. Over the years, as she had risen in her career, she had made a serious effort to dress in a more mature fashion. People took you seriously when your clothes were clean and pressed. If she still wore sweatpants, jeans worn through at the knees, and overly large T-shirts at home, well, that could be excused.

"Maybe it was that Clare who was a good influence on you," Ellen went on.

"Mom was a good influence on Clare, too, Grandma," Tamsin said. "Mom and her other friend, Danielle. They both helped Clare leave her awful fiancé way back when. They helped give her the courage."

"Breaking an engagement is a serious matter," Ellen said with a little frown.

"And Clare left him at the altar!" Tamsin added.

Gincy cringed. "That wasn't my idea, Mom, I swear. I was as shocked as anyone."

"It must have been like in a movie! What was that one with Julia Roberts like, a century ago? *Runaway Bride* or something?"

"Was he really an awful man?" Ellen asked.

"Yes, Mom," Gincy said, "he was awful and mean-spirited. Clare would have been miserable being married to him."

Ellen gave a firm nod. "Then you and Danielle did the right thing. Virginia? Thank you for the little village."

"Glad you like it, Mom," Gincy said. "Really."

Ellen, having said her peace, arranged the candy canes to her liking, and pronounced on her daughter's decent appearance, went off to the kitchen.

There was no doubt about it, Gincy thought, picking up the unidentified crocheted object and turning it in her hand as Tamsin had done. Her mother had improved since the unexpected arrival of her daughter and granddaughter. Their presence seemed to have nudged her back to some interest in life, and she had already gained back a few pounds. Maybe it would be all right to leave Appleville in the next day or two.

Gincy was no saint or martyr. She missed her husband, and though she knew he would join her at her mother's for Christmas Day if she asked, bringing Justin with him, she would rather be home, under her own roof, in her own pleasant home.

And why else, she thought, glancing at the candy cane her mother had insisted on hanging herself—the right way—why else would her mother have asked twice how long she and Tamsin were planning to stay unless she was prepared for them to leave? No doubt Ellen Gannon wanted her home back under her own control, now that she had regained some of her old spirit along with her appetite. That was understandable. She was a proud and independent woman. *I'm like her in that way*, Gincy thought. *As in so many other ways.*

Well, maybe they would leave the following day, Christmas Eve. Or maybe they would stay through Christmas morning. Yes, that was a better idea. She would ask Tommy to come by Number Nineteen, and she would make her mother and her brother a big Christmas breakfast—no runny eggs or too crispy bacon, maybe pancakes instead, and not with lumps—and see them settled with plenty of good, easy-to-prepare food in the house for a decent Christmas dinner—no prepackaged frozen meals or fast food. And then she and Tamsin would set out for Boston, where they would spend the afternoon and evening celebrating as a family with Rick and Justin.

Whatever she decided, she knew she would be back in Appleville some time in January—after her birthday on the first, which she would definitely spend in Boston, no doubt exuberantly thanking Rick for whatever it was she found in that little box already under their tree. She would be back to Appleville to confirm that Tommy was all right and that her mother wasn't once again sliding into depression and lethargy. No more six-month intervals between visits. And she would call her mother every other day and her brother once a week. She would make it a point.

"Mom?"

Tamsin's voice brought her back from her reverie. "What?" she said.

"What are you doing to that thing?"

Gincy frowned and looked down at the crocheted object

still in her hand. She was gripping it by what might be its neck.

"It looks like you're strangling it," Tamsin said. "You shouldn't strangle the family's Christmas snake."

Gincy laughed and tossed the thing to her daughter. "Don't ever let your father see that," she said. "You know how he feels about snakes."

CHAPTER 39

It was late afternoon and the sky was steadily darkening. The three women were gathered in the living room, Gincy and Tamsin on the couch and Ellen in what had always been "her chair," a high-backed armchair bought on sale at one of those big-box furniture stores a good twenty-five years earlier.

"The tree looks very nice, Virginia," Ellen said.

Gincy, who was checking her office e-mail, looked up from her laptop and smiled. While it certainly couldn't compare to her neighbors' potted trees with their theme decorations, the old Gannon family tree did have a sort of charm, even if it was indefinable.

"We need some Christmas music," Tamsin announced, and she got up from the couch.

Gincy and Rick had given her parents a CD player years earlier; Ellen had been suspicious—"The radio has always been fine for me"—but Ed had taken to it and over time had amassed a decent collection of music, including some popular jazz, big band favorites, and the much loved Christmas standards.

"This one's got a cute cover," Tamsin said, loading a CD. "Bing Crosby, whoever he is."

After a few fairly secular ballads, the opening bars of "God Rest Ye Merry, Gentlemen" sounded through the living room. When the chorus came along, Gincy found herself quietly singing along with Bing's famous bass baritone.

"Oh, tidings of comfort and joy . . ."

Ellen sighed.

Gincy looked up from her laptop. Her mother's expression was wistful. "What's wrong, Mom?" she asked.

Ellen put her hand briefly to her heart. "Nothing," she said. "It's just that this was your father's favorite Christmas carol."

"That's right, Mom. I remember him singing it. He had such a good voice when he was younger. So clear. A lovely tenor."

"I remember Grandpa singing, too," Tamsin said. "All sorts of songs. What was that goofy, really ancient song—something about a cement mixer and putty? It used to make me laugh so hard."

"That's why he sang it," Gincy said. "He loved to hear you laugh. Other people being happy made him happy."

"That's probably why he gave me a teddy bear every time he saw me," Tamsin said. "He knew how much I love teddy bears. Now I feel like I'm going to cry."

Gincy put her arm around her daughter's shoulder. "We all miss him," she said. "Right, Mom?"

But Ellen didn't answer. Instead she rose from her chair and went off in the direction of the kitchen. For a moment Gincy thought that maybe she shouldn't have tried to include her mother in the conversation. Then again, Ellen had been the one to mention the carol being Ed's favorite. Her mother was probably fine, just a bit melancholy. Even for the happiest, most content of people, Christmas could bring moments of poignant sadness as well as moments of great joy.

A few minutes later, Gincy and Tamsin heard a cry come from the kitchen.

"Grandma!" Tamsin shouted

"Stay here unless I call for you," Gincy told her daughter, literally tossing her laptop aside as she leapt up from the couch. As she hurried toward the kitchen she pulled her phone from her pocket, prepared to call 911.

"My, God, Mom," she cried, "what's happened?"

Her mother stood slumped against the counter, weeping and whimpering. On the cutting board behind her were two peeled potatoes, one of which had been sliced in half. And one of her mother's dull knives sat next to it, a tiny spot of blood on the blade.

In two strides Gincy was at her mother's side, lifting her hand. A quick glance at the wound assured Gincy that it was minor, and therefore completely out of proportion to the reaction it had elicited. She led her mother to the sink, where she ran the damaged fingertip under warm water and then, with a clean paper towel, dried it. Her own hands were shaking slightly, not from the sight of blood. No. Her hands were shaking because never, not in the fifty years she had known her mother, had she ever seen her cry. She was shocked. She was frightened.

"Here, Mom," she said, "let's sit down." She led her mother to the table and helped her to sit in her usual place. Tears were still streaming down Ellen's face, and little whimpering sounds were still coming from her throat. There was no box of tissues at hand, so Gincy grabbed a few paper napkins from the plastic holder that lived on the table and pressed them into her mother's hand.

"I'll get a Band-Aid," she said. She knew there was a box

in one of the drawers she had cleaned and organized just the other day. A moment later, the small wound safely covered, Gincy leaned down and put her arms around her mother's hunched shoulders.

"Don't leave me, Virginia," Ellen sobbed. "Not yet. Please."

Gincy was stunned. How had her mother known she was planning to go back to Boston on Christmas Day? But maybe that wasn't what her mother had meant at all. "I'm right here, Mom," she said, gently smoothing her mother's thin hair. "I'm not going anywhere."

"You're all I have left, Virginia. Now that your father is gone."

Gincy swallowed hard. She could choose to take this the wrong way. She could choose to believe that what her mother really meant was not "I love you and I need you" but "You're my last choice but you're better than nothing."

She chose to believe the first. Above all, she thought, be kind.

And she remembered what she had been thinking the other day at dinner. She had been thinking that maybe her mother had been holding her grief so tightly to herself because she was afraid of its power if unleashed. Well, something seemed to have unleashed it.

"Sometimes," her mother said through her tears, "I feel that I can't go on without him. . . ."

Gincy became aware that Tamsin was standing in the doorway, her face drawn with concern. She shook her head and managed a small smile. Tamsin turned away.

"When I found him that morning," Ellen went on, "I felt as if my life were over. I had made his breakfast, like I always did. I just wanted to see why he hadn't come into the kitchen yet, so I went back to the bedroom. He was alive when I got up. I know he was. I heard him breathing.

I saw him. I saw his eyelids flutter. But when I went back, only half an hour later . . ."

Gincy felt her legs begin to go out from under her, and she grabbed the back of the closest chair and sank into it. Her head began to spin and she thought she might be sick. She had never asked about the details of that awful morning. Her father had died in his sleep; of course her mother had been the one to find him! She had known that, of course she had, but somehow she had managed to block the horrible image from her mind, the image of her mother standing by the side of the bed she had shared with her beloved husband for over fifty years, alone and helpless with his body. The shame pressed down on Gincy, a terrible weight. She reached over and took her mother's hand. She found that she couldn't speak.

"I loved him from the first day we met," Ellen went on, her voice trembling. "And there he was, just gone from me. I wanted to lie down next to him and just . . . just slip away. There are days still when all I want to do is die so that we can be together again." Ellen looked up, her eyes searching her daughter's face. "But here I am, still alive. I don't understand. Why? Why am I still here?"

Gincy tightened her grip on her mother's hand and looked her squarely in the eye. "Because we need you here, Mom," she said, her voice trembling. "Me and Tommy and Justin and Tamsin. We need you."

Ellen wiped her eyes with the soggy napkins. "Your father always told me that I could rely on you when he was gone. He said I could ask you for help if he died before me. But I didn't want to ask you for help. I didn't want to ask anyone, especially not you. I didn't want you to think I was weak. I didn't want you to think badly of me, you Virginia, of all people."

Gincy shook her head as tears cascaded down her cheeks. "Mom, you stubborn old thing. We're so much alike, you and I. Asking for help when you really need it is the smart thing to do. It's the courageous thing to do. We've both had to learn that the hard way. Dad would be so glad that we're here, together, finally."

And then, Gincy thought of the life-changing moment twenty years before when she told Rick that, yes, she would move in with him and Justin. It was not what she had planned to say. She had gone to Rick's apartment to break up with him because she was so afraid of taking the emotional chance, so afraid of the risk involved with committing herself to another person. So afraid of love. But then, standing before the man she loved and admired, she had found the courage to accept his offer. She remembered thinking, "The necessary leap of faith. Someone had to take it." Rick had taken the leap, and she had followed.

Now Ellen Gannon was the one who had found the courage to take the leap of faith and share her grief with her daughter. *And I'll follow*, Gincy thought. She would accept her mother's gift and try to make up for not having been brave enough to establish a better relationship with her before now.

"I'm so sorry, Mom," she said, her voice thick with emotion. "I'm so sorry for not really listening, for not really seeing. I'm sorry for everything. I want to make it up to you. I *will* make it up to you."

Ellen coughed and blew her nose. "Let me get you some water, Mom." Gincy let go of her mother's hand and went to the sink. And she remembered with shame that she used to consider her mother a failure. That was the word she had used over and over, a failure. And now, now she was mortified that she could have been so immature and blind to her mother's achievements. What were those achievements? To truly love and care for her husband. To be the best mother she knew how to be.

What higher achievement was there, really, than to love another person with all of your heart and soul?

"Why don't you sit with Tamsin while I finish getting dinner ready," she said, handing her mother the glass of water. "Do you think you'll be able to eat something?"

Ellen took a long drink and then sniffed loudly. "Yes, Virginia," she said. "I think I can manage something."

CHAPTER 40

"Rick." Gincy sighed in relief. "I'm so glad you picked up."

"Are you all right?" he asked. "What's going on?"

"Something happened, Rick. In fact, it happened just a few minutes ago. It was horrible, but it was wonderful at the same time. Do you know what I mean?"

"I think so, yes. But maybe you'd better give me the details. You sound a bit shaky. Should I be concerned? Are you sitting down?"

"No. I'm in the backyard. I need the fresh air. I felt pretty awful earlier, but I'm all right now."

And she told her husband what had happened.

"It was the first time I'd ever seen my mother cry, Rick," she said. "I'm not sure I'll ever be the same, and I think that might be a good thing."

"Oh, Gincy," Rick said. "I wish I were there with you right now."

"You are with me, Rick," Gincy assured him. "Always. And you were right. My mother does need me. I never really believed it until today. And she just couldn't bring herself to tell me." Gincy laughed. "And to think it was Bing Crosby who did the trick."

"How does she seem now?" Rick asked.

"Subdued, but okay. Still, I have a favor to ask you, and it's a big one. Rick, will you come to Appleville for Christmas? Justin, too? Will you ask him? Mom needs us all, I think, not just me. She needs to know that she has us, that just because she's lost Dad she's not alone. And I think that Tommy needs us all, too."

"Of course I'll be there," Rick said. "And I'll call Justin later this evening. I'm proud of you for what you're doing for your mother, and for Tommy."

"Don't say that!" Gincy cried. "You know I feel weird when someone tells me they're proud of me. I feel like a fraud, like I'm putting something over on people."

Rick laughed. "Okay. Look, why don't I bring a few bags of tempting goodies from the North End. And some good wine. It sounds like you could use a nice Merlot. And I'll arrange a turkey. Someone must still have one for sale."

"That sounds like a great idea. And bring a decent roasting pan and our essential knives. My mother's kitchen equipment is in pretty bad shape. Just don't slice a hand off with the knives while you're packing them, please."

"I haven't cut myself with a kitchen knife since . . . What was it, a month ago?"

"Six weeks," she said. "And there's Tommy's truck. Have Justin take a look at it when he gets here, will you? I'm not sure Tommy should be driving it in its current condition. But I know he doesn't have the money for repairs or to buy a new one."

"We'll take care of that," Rick assured her. "The guy needs wheels. He has to feel independent."

"And a coat. He needs a decent winter coat. Do you still have that parka you bought and then decided didn't fit you properly?" Gincy asked. "The one we couldn't return because you had lost the receipt? Or did it make it to Goodwill already?"

"I've got it. It should fit Tommy."

"And one more thing," Gincy said. "Mom's feeling pretty overwhelmed at the moment. I think that you and Justin should stay at the little bed-and-breakfast in town, assuming they have a room. I think it might be easier on her, not having a crowd in the house. Is that all right?"

"Whatever makes things easier for *you*, Gincy. I'll call the place as soon as we get off the phone."

"Thank you. Rick? I can't wait to see you."

"I'll be there before you know it," he promised.

"Good," Gincy said, looking up at the old bare maple in the corner of the yard. "Good."

CHAPTER 41

After dinner, at which Ellen had eaten heartily, Gincy once again got her mother settled in the living room with Tamsin by her side. Gincy had told Tamsin what had transpired earlier; she knew she could trust Tamsin to do and say the right and comforting thing. She was, after all, Rick's daughter. And there was an old black-and-white version of *A Christmas Carol* on television. It would keep them occupied for a while, assuming the Ghost of Christmas Past didn't send Ellen into another emotional meltdown.

Gincy retreated again to the kitchen and called Danielle.

"Look," she said, once again without a greeting, "I'd like to take my mother on a cruise."

"To whom am I speaking?"

"Ha, ha. Seriously, you've been on a million cruises."

"Five," Danielle corrected.

"Whatever. Can you give me some advice about choosing an appropriate line or destination? I'm clueless, and I don't trust online travel services."

"What's been going on up there in Appleville?" Danielle

asked. "One day you're talking about matricide and the next day you're going on vacation with your mother."

"Things have changed."

"Well, I'm glad to hear it. Am I going to get the details?"

"Yes," Gincy said, "but not now."

"I could come with you two, if you decide you need the support," Danielle offered. "I could work on my tan while you and your mother bond over yoga classes or tango lessons."

Gincy laughed. "We'll see. In the meantime, can you help me out?"

"Sure," Danielle promised. "I'll do some research and send you my recommendations for a cruise Ellen would enjoy."

"Nothing raunchy, please," Gincy warned. "No swinging singles."

Danielle laughed. "Seriously? Do you think I'd send the formidable Ellen Gannon on a swinging singles cruise?"

"Maybe it's what she needs."

"Gincy. Behave."

"I'm trying," she said, "believe me. And guess what my brilliant daughter engineered the other day? A mercy visit from Clare."

"Let me guess. It really did turn out to be a mercy visit, didn't it?"

"Absolutely," Gincy told her. "Clare was like a ministering angel or something. At least, that's how my mother saw her. Clare managed to work a few minor miracles for me."

"That's our Clare, all right. Hey, you know what I remembered the other day?" Danielle asked. "Remember the time that first summer when I asked you and Clare to name your favorite television show, movie, designer, and cocktail? I thought it would be a way for us to get to know each other."

Gincy frowned. "No. I don't remember. What did I say?"

"You said, *The Honeymooners*, *Cool Hand Luke*, and something made with gin. Of course, if I had known you better I wouldn't have bothered to ask about a favorite designer."

Gincy laughed. "What was I back then, a guy? Well, I do still like gin on occasion. What did you say?"

"That's the odd thing," Danielle said. "I have no idea. And I don't remember Clare's answer, either. All I remember is your answer."

"That's because it was so weird!"

"Have a merry Christmas, Gincy."

"You, too, Danielle. Well, you know what I mean."

"I do," Danielle said. "My girls would kill us if we didn't put up a tree along with the menorah. And buy them presents, of course."

"Of course," Gincy said. "Who doesn't like presents?"

CHAPTER 42

"We've got a big surprise for you, Grandma," Tamsin said at breakfast on Christmas Eve morning.

"Now, I know you don't usually like surprises, Mom," Gincy said quickly, before her mother could protest. "But I think you'll like this one. Rick and Justin will be joining us later today and they'll be here through Christmas."

Ellen smiled and put down her spoon. She had eaten all of the oatmeal Gincy had prepared for her, along with a piece of the homemade coffee cake Adele Brown had dropped off earlier.

"That *is* a nice surprise," she said. "I haven't seen either of them since . . . since your father's funeral. But where will I put them? There's Tommy's old room, but it's so small. . . . They'll be so crowded in there. . . ."

"Rick and Justin will stay at the bed-and-breakfast on Main Street," Gincy told her. "Luckily, there was a cancellation. And we'll take care of everything, Mom. You don't have to lift a finger. I'll even wash the dishes after Christmas dinner."

"You hated washing the dishes when you were young, Virginia," Ellen said with a frown. "And you were very bad at it. I always had to rewash at least half of the glass-ware."

Gincy smiled. "I still hate it, but I think I've done okay these past few days, haven't I? Still, I'm lucky to have a dishwasher at home."

"But sometimes she doesn't load the dishwasher right," Tamsin said. "Sorry, Mom, but sometimes you don't. The stuff in the top basket comes out with gunk on it."

"I'm sure your mother does her best," Ellen said.

Tamsin, looking a bit chastened, announced that she was off to take a shower.

Alone with her mother, Gincy felt awkward, almost shy. At least she knew enough not to refer directly to yester-day's . . . incident. "How is the cut?" she asked. "Did you change the Band-Aid this morning?"

"Yes. It's healing nicely. Thank you, Virginia."

Gincy brought the breakfast plates, bowls, and cups to the sink. With her back to her mother she asked, "So, you're feeling better, Mom?"

"Yes, Virginia," Ellen said firmly. "I'm feeling better."

"Your first Christmas without Dad," Gincy said gently, turning once again to face her mother. "You must have so many good memories of all your years together."

"I do. And it's your first Christmas without your father. I know you miss him, too."

"I do," Gincy said. "Mom, just so you know. Tommy will be okay. I mean, Rick and I have talked . . ."

"I know what you mean. Thank you, Virginia. And Vir-ginia? I don't think your brother needs to know . . ."

"Of course not, Mom," Gincy said. "Of course not."

Around eleven that morning a huge box arrived from what Gincy recognized as a high-end specialty online shop.

It was addressed to Mrs. Ellen Gannon. Gincy carried it into the kitchen and placed it on the table.

"Boy, this thing is heavy!" she said.

"What on earth is that?" Ellen asked. "I didn't order anything."

"It's from my friend Danielle and her family," she said. "Do you want me to open it for you?"

Ellen did, so Gincy picked up a kitchen knife and with some difficulty sliced through the tape sealing the cardboard. Inside was a large wicker basket chock full of boxes of candies and bottles of wines and packages of dried fruits and other delectable treats.

"Oh, look," Tamsin cried. "Cheese straws! I love cheese straws. Can I have one, Grandma?"

"Of course." Ellen shook her head. "How will I ever eat all of this?" she asked.

Gincy refrained from laughing. "I'm sure you'll manage, Mom. And we're here to help."

Not minutes later the doorbell rang again, and Gincy, half suspecting what might be waiting on the doorstep, went to answer it. She was right. It was a gift from Clare and her family. This time it was a gorgeous array of white roses and green pine boughs and red carnations, all tied with a red, green, and gold plaid ribbon. She figured that Danielle had told Clare about her breakthrough with her mother. The extravagant gifts were her friends' way of offering congratulations to both women.

"Those friends of yours shouldn't have spent so much money on me," Ellen said, shaking her head again and gently touching the petals of one of the fat roses. "That Clare would have made a lovely bridesmaid if you had had a real wedding here in Appleville, Virginia."

Gincy rolled her eyes. "Have a chocolate, Mom."

"Well, if you say so." Ellen selected a candy from the box she had already opened. "Um," she said, after taking a bite. "Caramel. My favorite. I think I'll have another."

Rick arrived at Number Nineteen just after the women had finished lunch. Ellen greeted him in her usual way, as if he were a hero returning from a great and mighty battle. This used to bother Gincy; she used to think her mother was deliberately pointing out the vast difference between her opinion of her daughter and her opinion of her son-in-law. But this time, her mother's enthusiastic response to Rick's presence made her smile. After all, she too pretty much thought of Rick as a hero, and had ever since the time twenty years ago when he had come to her rescue in the middle of the night when she thought someone was trying to break into her apartment. In the end the would-be burglar was just Mrs. Norton, her poor, addled neighbor, who had confused Gincy's apartment with her own. Gincy had been mortified by her show of fear and weakness and had expected the worst from her new boyfriend. But Rick had kept the incident to himself and had never once teased her about it. Another reason to fall in love.

Justin arrived shortly after his father. He was engulfed in his sister's embrace before his grandmother greeted him with almost as much praise and adulation as she had his father.

Gincy's initial thought on meeting Justin for the first time all those years ago was that he was his father's Mini-Me, a being who had sprouted from the forehead of the one parent without the addition of someone else's DNA. Over the years, though, she had seen Justin grow into some of his birth mother's physical characteristics; for example, he was several inches taller than his father, as his mother had been. Today he was wearing dark jeans, beautiful brown lace-up shoes, and a tab collar shirt of heavy cotton. The interest in style was another thing Justin had gotten from Annie. Photographs of Rick's first wife all showed a well-put-together young woman with a flare for wearing long silk scarves and big hoop earrings. That is, until the cancer that had killed her at such a young age first robbed her of her joie de vivre.

"I'll call Uncle Tommy," Tamsin said, "and let him know that everyone is here."

"How are the accommodations?" Gincy asked her husband when Justin had gone off with his grandmother to look at the Christmas tree and especially the little Victorian village Ellen genuinely seemed to love.

"Fine," he said. "It's a nice little place. I could only get us one room, but at least there are two beds. You know how Justin tosses and turns all night. I don't know how his girlfriends stand it."

Gincy didn't like to think about Justin and his girlfriends in bed, but she let the remark go. "Look, Rick," she said. "I had an idea. I'd like to take my mother on a cruise. It doesn't have to be super high-end—I don't think Mom would like that and we probably couldn't afford it—but it has to be nice. I've already asked Danielle to help me find the right sort of package."

"I think it's a great idea," he said. "And maybe I'll ask Tommy to stay with Tamsin and me in Boston while you and your mother are away. He is my brother-in-law. It's about time I took some responsibility for him. Well, you know what I mean. Showed him some real friendship."

Gincy frowned. "But what would you do with him?"

"We'll hang out," Rick said with a shrug. "We could catch a Red Sox game or a hockey or a basketball game. I could take him to the museum."

"Tommy, at the Museum of Fine Arts? Trolleys, yes. History paintings, not so much. He'll be bored out of his mind."

"Now, Gincy," Rick scolded. "You're doing it again. Give the guy the benefit of the doubt. Besides, everyone loves ancient Egyptian stuff. Mummies, buried treasure, Cleopatra. He'll have fun."

"You're right," Gincy said. "Above all, be kind. It's my new mantra. And look, Rick, I promised Mom this morning that we're committed to looking out for Tommy in the future."

"Good. We won't let him fall through the cracks. So many people get lost."

"He wouldn't be happy in Boston," she said, "so somehow we'll have to make sure he's safe and settled in Appleville. We could talk to people who might be willing to give him a full-time job he could handle. Maybe Harriman's could take him back. I get the feeling he's become too scared or defeatist to even try for a decent position. And I don't think he's ridiculously proud. I think he might welcome our help in getting him a job he likes and not see it as charity. At least, I hope he would welcome our help."

"And," Rick said, "we might be able to afford to buy him a small apartment, or to pay his rent if we can't find a decent place to buy. But I don't think there's any rush to make decisions about Tommy's future. I don't think your mother is going anywhere yet."

Gincy smiled. "You think she's got a new lease on life?"

"Something like that. At least we can hope that she does. And don't worry, I'll approach Tommy when the time seems right about what Ellen is giving him in the way of money."

"I love you, Rick," Gincy said, throwing her arms around her husband. "Do you know that?"

Rick hugged her back. "I do know that," he said. "I've never doubted it for a second."

"I was thinking, Rick," Gincy said. "There's this local restaurant Mom and Dad used to like. At least, I know they went there a few times over the years. Maybe we all could go there for dinner tonight. I, for one, could use a break from cooking—you know I don't really enjoy it, and this kitchen is archaic. That is, if Mom wants to go out."

"Sure. It could be fun. Why don't you ask her?"

"It's nothing fancy," she said, thinking of the Red Rose in Commons Corner. "In fact, it's pretty much the antithesis of fancy. Not that that bothers *me*."

"Rats," Rick said. "And here I brought my tuxedo."

CHAPTER 43

Gincy was surprised to learn that not only did her mother very much want to have dinner that evening at the Country Store but also that she had been wanting to have dinner there since her husband died. But because eating alone in public was out of the question for a woman like Ellen Gannon, she had not been to the restaurant since May.

"Your father and I went to the Country Store for dinner the first Saturday of every month for the past twenty-five years," Ellen told her daughter. It was another nail in the coffin of Gincy's formerly held notion that her parents had had an unhappy marriage.

"This place looks like fun," Tamsin said when the family was gathered at the hostess station.

"Are the waiters and waitresses dressed in . . ." Justin watched as a young woman in vaguely eighteenth-century garb—complete with long dress, apron, and mobcap—passed by carrying an enormous tray of empty plates on her shoulder. "Yep," he said. "Just what I thought."

The Country Store. Long wooden tables with benches instead of chairs. Wooden barrels full of apples (plastic, Gincy suspected), spinning wheels, bales of hay, metal buckets of all sizes hanging from walls and posts, an oil lantern on every table, and peanut shells scattered across the floor. The décor might have been a nod to an idealized countrified past, but the menu was decidedly twenty-first century—burgers, nachos, triple-decker sandwiches, pizza, and chicken nuggets.

"I used to come here," Tommy said when the family was seated. "Back when I was with Kate."

Gincy smiled at her brother. "And what was your favorite thing to order?" she asked.

"The onion blossom. Look, it's still here on the menu!"

"Is it big enough to share?" Tamsin asked.

"It's huge," Tommy assured her. "I'll get one and we can all eat it. But I'm going to get a burger, too."

Their waitress arrived shortly after and introduced herself as Stacy. "It's good to see you, Mrs. Gannon," she said. "The usual?"

"Yes, please. The beef pot pie. I just love the beef pot pie here."

"I think I'll get that, too, Grandma," Tamsin said.

Tommy, seated to the right of his sister, leaned in and whispered. "What happened to Mom? She seems so much better. What did you say to her?"

Gincy shrugged. "I didn't say anything. I guess the Christmas season worked its magic."

"Well, whatever happened, I'm glad. I was starting to think she'd . . ."

"Tommy," Gincy said, "I think Mom will be with us for a good long while. Hey, I remembered something when Tamsin and I were decorating Mom's tree. Do you remember the time we made those Christmas ornaments out of Styrofoam and glitter? And we started throwing around the glitter and squeezing the bottles of glue all over the place? You were really young, so maybe you don't remember."

"I remember." Tommy laughed. "We got in so much trouble. Well, mostly it was you who got in trouble. Mom was like, Virginia, you're the older one, you should have known better."

Gincy shrugged. "I guess I should have. But we did have fun, didn't we?"

"Yeah," Tommy said. "We did. But you know what? I don't remember who started throwing stuff around."

Gincy smiled. "Neither do I, but I guess it doesn't matter." *All that matters*, she thought, *was that Tommy and I remember being together.*

There was much laughter over the course of the meal, first when Tommy's onion blossom arrived and proved to be large enough to feed twenty people, then when Justin recounted the antics of his roommate's new puppy—"I swear his paws are bigger than his head, and he's constantly tripping over his own ears"—and, of course, when Rick managed to squirt ketchup all over his shirt. "It's not a night out," he said, ineffectually wiping at the stain, "without me ruining a shirt."

When they had all eaten their fill and more and it was time to pay the bill, their waitress told them that the owner of the restaurant had taken care of the cost of Ellen's meal. "We're just happy to have you back, Mrs. Gannon," she said. "Now, try not to be a stranger."

Tommy patted his mother's hand. "We could come together, Mom," he said. "I mean, if you want."

"I think that would be nice," Ellen said. "Thank you, Tommy."

Rick and Justin split the bill. "I make decent money, Dad," Justin said when his father protested. "It's not a problem." After the bill had been paid, father and son went back to the bed-and-breakfast, Rick in his Volvo wagon and Justin in his two-year-old BMW. Tommy got in his truck and headed out, after promising to be at Number Nineteen for breakfast Christmas morning. Gincy got behind the wheel of her car, Ellen beside her and Tamsin in the back-seat.

"Put on your seat belt, Mom," Gincy said, as she started the engine.

"You're very bossy, Virginia," her mother replied.

Gincy smiled into the winter dark. "I know," she said. "I got it from you."

"Grandma?" Tamsin said. "You want to go to church tomorrow, right?"

"Of course," Ellen said firmly. "Why in the world wouldn't I?"

"Good. You—I mean, we'll all see your friends again."

"It was almost a perfect evening, wasn't it, Virginia?" Ellen Gannon said after a moment. Her tone was unmis-takably nostalgic but not sad.

"Yes, Mom," Gincy replied, eyes on the road. "Almost perfect."

CHAPTER 44

It was Christmas morning and the family, including Tommy, was gathered in the house in which Gincy Gannon had grown up. The house from which she had been desperate to escape. At the moment, she thought, looking around the kitchen table with the permanently sticky cloth, Number Nineteen—and the people who had once lived there and the person who lived there still—didn't seem so bad at all.

Ellen had insisted on making breakfast for everyone, and though the result was the usual not-so-good—edible if not enticing—at least she accomplished the entire meal on her own without incident. It was another step in the right direction.

Afterward, Tamsin and Gincy cleaned up, under Ellen's unnecessary directions.

"Virginia," she ordered, "don't use that sponge. Use this one."

"Okay, Mom." After all, Gincy thought, wiping the counter next to the sink, it was her mother's house. She had the right to be in charge.

"And Tamsin, check that your mother has thoroughly washed the glasses."

"Yes, Grandma."

When Ellen was satisfied that her daughter wasn't going to make more of a mess than she had set out to clean up, she announced that she was off to take a shower.

Justin, accompanied by Tommy, went to start on the list of minor repairs of the sort that his grandfather would normally have handled—the chores beyond Gincy's rudimentary skills.

"I'm not much good with my hands," Tommy said before they set out from the kitchen. "I won't be of much help."

Justin, carrying his grandfather's toolbox, smiled. "Sure you will, Tommy. A job is always easier with a buddy along. And you can hold the level for me. It's what I used to do for Grandpa."

"There's an extra branch."

Justin shook his head. "What do you mean?"

"When I put the Christmas tree together, there was a branch left over. I couldn't figure out where it goes."

Justin laughed. "Happens all the time. We'll figure it out together."

When they had gone off, Gincy sighed. "Seeing those two together," she said to her husband, "it's such a contrast. Justin has so much, and Tommy, well, he has so little."

Rick turned from Ellen's wonky stove, where he had been fiddling with the oven controls. "He has us," he pointed out. "And I think we're better than nothing."

I hope so, Gincy thought. "You know, Rick," she said, as he continued to battle with the oven controls, "I've realized that I have to take care of Mom for Dad's sake if for nothing else. He loved my mother, I know he did. And she loved him. There's good in her. I've finally seen and acknowledged that. And," she added, picking up the frying pan and eyeing it warily, "I have *got* to get her some new cookware! The bottom on this is almost eaten through. What has she been doing to it? Cleaning it with acid?"

"At the very least we have to get her a new oven," Rick said with a frown. "If this thing gets up to temperature by the time we're back from church, I'll be a monkey's uncle. But we'll wait until her birthday in February. You know how she is. If we try to give her a big gift at any other time but a holiday, she'll see it as charity and refuse it."

Gincy laughed. "You're so right. Which is why I'm pretty sure she'll accept our gift of a cruise only if we emphasize that it's a Christmas present."

At ten o'clock the family gathered in the living room. Ellen sat in the middle of the couch, rather than in her usual armchair, her children on either side of her. Rick perched on the arm of the couch, next to his wife. And then he yelped.

"What the blazes is that thing?" he said, pointing with a trembling finger at the brown and beige crocheted object sitting under the tree.

Tamsin scurried over and shoved the Christmas snake behind the Victorian village. "Nothing, Dad," she said. "Forget it."

Tamsin joined her brother on the floor. *Ah*, Gincy thought. *The suppleness of youth*. It wasn't the getting down that was so difficult. It was the getting back up again.

"Time for gifts," Tamsin announced.

Ellen frowned. "I'm afraid I never got around to shopping except for when Virginia's friend Clare took us to the fair at my church."

"Grandma," Tamsin said, "we're just happy to be here with you. That's your gift to us."

And, Gincy thought, there would be many more gifts to give and receive once the Luongo family was back home in

Boston. Her daughter was a truly good person, but she was as avaricious at heart as any teenage girl; weeks earlier she had given her parents an extensive wish list. And Justin had hinted that he had his eye on some new electronic gadget or other. Rick had seen to that. Her children would not be disappointed, and neither would her husband when he saw that she had gotten him tickets to a revival of *Amadeus*, one of his favorite plays. And there was that new brown leather blazer waiting for her to try on and just possibly a Georgian fede ring. . . .

Justin reached up and took his grandmother's hand. "Grandma, Uncle Tommy showed me that new frame Grandpa was making for your grandmother's mirror. I'd like to finish it for you, if that's okay. I'm not saying I'm as good a woodworker as Grandpa was, but he did teach me everything I know."

"That would be wonderful, Justin," Ellen said. "Thank you."

Rick wiped a tear from his eye. "That's our boy," he whispered to Gincy.

Tamsin handed her grandmother a small package tied with a red ribbon. "I saw you looking at this at the Christmas fair," she said, "but I knew you wouldn't buy it for yourself, so I got it for you when you weren't looking."

Ellen carefully removed the ribbon and wrapping paper from the package. Her mother, Gincy thought, would trim off any ragged edge and use the paper again. Well, thrift wasn't a bad thing. What had her father always said? Waste not, want not.

It was an embroidered eyeglass case. "Thank you, Tamsin," Ellen said. "I was admiring this. The case I have is falling apart. I've mended it twice but . . ."

Tamsin turned to Tommy. "And Uncle Tommy? We got you a membership at the trolley museum! They're sending you your membership card in the mail. And your engineer's hat!"

Gincy had never seen her brother so flustered, and it moved her. "I don't know what to say," he began. "It's like . . . They have that course where you get to drive a trolley . . . and they're getting a new streetcar next spring, all the way from England."

Ellen handed her son the bulky package she had asked Justin to pass to her from its place under the tree. Tommy tore open the paper to reveal the hand-knit mittens Ellen had bought for him at the fair.

"Now, try not to lose them, will you?" Ellen said, retrieving the torn wrapping paper her son had scattered.

"Yes, Mom," Tommy said. "I'll try."

Gincy shifted on the couch to look directly at her mother. "There's one more thing, Mom," she said.

Ellen frowned. "What have you done, Virginia? Did you forget to defrost the turkey?"

Gincy laughed. "You're incorrigible, you know that? No, Mom, the turkey is fine. Rick saw to that when he picked it up from the butcher's yesterday on his way into town. What I want to say is that I'd like to take you on a cruise, anywhere you'd like to go. It's your Christmas present from us all, so you can't say no."

Ellen's eyes lit up. "I most certainly will not say no! How did you know I've always wanted to go on a cruise?"

Gincy glanced over at her brother. "A little birdie told me."

Tommy, still holding his new mittens, smiled.

"I'll need some nice new clothes," Ellen announced. "A few lightweight skirts and blouses. And do they dress up for dinner, I wonder."

"I'll take you shopping, Mom," Gincy promised. "There are some nice shops at the mall in Newington."

Ellen waved her hand dismissively. "Don't bother with

that! My sewing machine still works and I have some lovely fabric I've been putting aside for years. When are we going? It doesn't matter. I'll get started right away! And you could probably use some nice clothes too, Virginia. Even if you are less wrinkled than you used to be, I've seen some of the things you like to wear. Don't tell me you still have those awful old blue jeans, the ones with the hole in the seat."

"You wore jeans with a hole in the seat?" Rick whispered. "Wish I'd been around to see that."

Gincy playfully slapped her husband's leg. "Not since I was twenty-two, Mom."

"And I have all of my old brochures . . ."

"We'll need up-to-date brochures, Mom. Danielle is helping us with that."

"You know, Virginia, if you had had a real wedding here in Appleville I could have met Danielle, too."

"I know, Mom."

"Virginia? Thank you. This is a wonderful Christmas."

Gincy briefly took her mother's hand. But only briefly. One step at a time.

Rick cleared his throat. "Tommy, I was thinking that when the girls are off sailing the high seas, you might like to visit Tamsin and me in Boston."

"We can ride the swan boats, Uncle Tommy."

Tommy looked decidedly nervous. "I'm not good on boats," he said. "I can't swim."

Tamsin laughed. "Oh, it's only a paddle boat and I think the water is, like, two feet deep. I promise you'll be fine. The ducks follow the boat, and we can feed them. It's fun. Except for when the seagulls try to muscle in on the poor little ducks. Once a seagull landed right next to my foot!"

Tommy shook his head. "I haven't been to Boston in almost fifteen years. It's probably changed a lot. I won't know my way around."

"You'll have Dad and Tamsin to help you negotiate," Justin said. "And depending on when you come, I'll see if I can squeeze in a visit, too."

Gincy smiled gratefully at her stepson. And she recalled the night so long ago when Tommy had showed up unannounced at her apartment in Boston with one of his degenerate buddies, looking for a place to party. The night Tommy and Rick, an unlikely pair, had first laid eyes on each other. To think they would all be here together, twenty years later, celebrating Christmas as a family . . .

"It's time to get ready for church," Ellen announced, pushing off the couch. "And we can't be late—it's terribly rude—so don't dawdle, Virginia."

"Okay, Mom," Gincy said. "I promise not to dawdle."

Chapter 45

Tommy drove his mother to the Church of the Risen Lord in her car; the rest of the family went in Rick's car. The Luongos weren't regular churchgoers, but for Ellen's sake—as well as for the memory of Ed Gannon— they were happy to make this Christmas Day appearance. Besides, Gincy thought, a little prayer never hurt anyone, not even an only occasional believer.

"I'm glad you thought to bring something nice for Mom and me to wear, Dad," Tamsin said from the backseat. "Who knew we were going to be in Appleville for Christmas."

Gincy smiled. "Yes, thanks, Rick. I totally forgot to ask you when we talked. I don't think Mom would have approved of our going to church in jeans and fleece jackets."

Rick sighed dramatically. "Just doing my job as Super Dad," he said. "And Super Husband."

The parking lot was almost entirely full by the time Rick pulled in. "That's what you like to see," he said. "A full house on Christmas."

Gincy, Rick, Justin, and Tamsin joined Ellen in the vestibule of the church. "Does Tommy often go to church with you, Mom?" Gincy asked, though Tommy had already told her the answer to that question. Her brother, holding the winter coat that Rick had given him privately that morning, was several feet away, talking to a man wearing a puffy orange jacket and camoflauge pants. Gincy thought he looked vaguely familiar. One of Tommy's old buddies maybe.

"Only when I ask him to," Ellen told her, as Tommy had done. "Except for today, I haven't asked him to come to church with me since your father died. But maybe it would be a good thing if I did."

"I think so, too, Mom," Gincy said. "I think it would be good for the both of you."

"Virginia?"

"Yes, Mom?"

"Thank you for giving Tommy the coat. I . . . For some reason I didn't know that he needed a new one. I haven't been as . . . as sharp lately as I might have been."

Gincy smiled at her mother. "You can't keep track of everything, Mom. And we have Rick to thank for the coat. If he hadn't lost the receipt so that we couldn't return it . . ."

"Virginia? About the cruise."

"You do still want to go?" Gincy asked. "I think we'll have a great time, Mom."

"Yes, it's not that." Mrs. Gannon glanced quickly around as if to be sure they weren't overheard. "I never told your father that I wanted to go on a cruise," she said. "I knew we couldn't afford it, and I didn't want him to feel badly about that."

Gincy's heart swelled, and she smiled at her mother. "That was kind of you, Mom," she said.

Tommy joined his family then. He had made an effort to look presentable but seemed ill at ease. Clearly dressing up—the old, ill-fitting suit jacket he had probably last worn at his father's funeral, with his usual jeans and T-shirt—made him uncomfortable. For the life of her Gincy couldn't remember if she had ever seen her brother in a tie. Not that it mattered. All that mattered was that Tommy was here, with his family.

The service was pleasant, Gincy thought, without any of the high church trappings like incense and pomp and circumstance and heavily embroidered robes that could serve to distract some people from the words of the Old and New Testament readings. The hymns, largely unfamiliar to Gincy, Rick, and their children, were sung with gusto by the congregation. And the sermon, given by Pastor Brown—*Another Brown!* Gincy thought with a smile— was remarkable for its clarity and its emphasis on what Pastor Brown called "the true essence of Christmas." And that, appropriately enough, was love. Just love.

Above all, Gincy thought, *be kind.*

It was so unbelievably simple.

When the service was over, Ellen seemed inclined to linger in the vestibule, where she proved to be a bit of a star. Gincy was pleased to see how many people came up to her mother to wish her well. Her mother seemed energized by the attention, and eager to introduce her family to those they hadn't already met at the Christmas fair or at her husband's funeral.

"Mr. Tyson! I'm so glad to see you, Merry Christmas. Meet my grandchildren."

"Mr. and Mrs. Clarke! This is my daughter, Virginia, the one I've told you all about. And this is her husband, Richard, and my grandchildren, Justin and Tamsin. Justin lives all on his own in Connecticut. He does something very important with money. And isn't Tamsin pretty? And she bakes very good sugar cookies."

"Mrs. Rogers! My daughter is taking me on a cruise! She's a big editor in Boston. She won a prize."

"Mrs. Garafalo, did you know that my Virginia was almost the very first baby born in Appleville in 1966? She came *this* close!"

Gincy nodded and said hello and shook hands when they were offered. And she was very glad that Tommy wasn't there to hear his mother go on; he had slipped away right after the service with the man in the puffy orange jacket. The fact that he had probably taken his mother's car was inconvenient. It meant that Ellen would have to sit in the backseat of Rick's car with her grandchildren. But Gincy wasn't going to make an issue of her brother's thoughtlessness. What mattered was that he not be there to hear his sister praised so lavishly, when after all he was a worthwhile person, too. He had been the one to note their mother's depression and to bring his sister home at long last. Gincy had never thought she would admit to this, but she had come to feel protective of her brother.

Tommy in his blue snowsuit with his adorable smile. Tommy hurting his head on the edge of the sandbox. Tommy, her partner in the glitter war. She wondered how much it would cost to get his tooth replaced.

When her mother turned to greet yet another member of the congregation, Gincy leaned into her husband. "Great," she said. "I'm a celebrity."

"Now, Gincy. Be nice."

"Sorry."

"Virginia." Ellen turned back to her daughter. "Mrs. Miller has invited me to her house for coffee and fruitcake. Her fruitcake is famous here in Appleville, you know. She'll drive me home well in time for Christmas dinner. Is that all right?"

"Of course, Mom," Gincy said. "Have a good time."

As Ellen went off with Mrs. Miller, another woman approached Gincy and introduced herself as Mrs. Buchanan.

"I saw you the other day," Gincy said. "At the fair."

"That's right. You were all with that lovely blond woman in the pretty pink coat. Well, I can't tell you how pleased we are to see your mother here today," she said. "After your father died, she stopped coming to our bridge games and she dropped out of the Altar Guild. You know, we do the flowers for the church and keep things nice and clean and polished. And recently she hasn't been to Sunday service, either. Anyway, we all called and stopped by the house, but she made it clear she wanted to be alone so, well, we stopped. We felt as if we were doing more harm than good. Maybe now she's finally ready to come back to us."

"I hope so," Gincy said. "And thank you for being concerned."

Mrs. Buchanan smiled. "It's easy to be concerned for someone like Ellen Gannon. She's just so nice."

Gincy watched Mrs. Buchanan bustle off, and then turned back to her husband and children.

"I'm hungry again," Tamsin announced. "I can't stop thinking of those cheese straws Danielle sent Grandma."

Gincy smiled and linked her arm with Rick's. "Then let's go home," she said.

CHAPTER 46

"Grandma was like a celebrity," Tamsin said, as the family drove back to Crescent Road. "I kept expecting someone to start taking pictures or something."

Justin nodded. "I think she liked being the center of attention, especially if what Mom says is true, that she's been in a sort of self-imposed exile since Grandpa died."

"Mom?" Tamsin asked. "Did you recognize that guy Tommy went off with after church?"

Gincy shook her head. "No. Well, not really." She looked over to her husband. "Can I really rely on Tommy to keep Mom fed and in good health?"

"Probably not," Rick said. "He'll do what he can, he loves her, but it probably won't be enough."

"He is what he is, Mom," Justin said.

"He does his best," Tamsin added. "He's got a good heart."

Gincy nodded. "I don't doubt that at all, not anymore."

"And he can burp the alphabet better than anyone I've ever met," Rick pointed out.

"I have to admit he is a good burper. And he was smart

enough to call me when he saw that Mom was failing. I've underestimated him all around."

You live, you learn, Gnicy thought. It was what her father always used to say.

"I hope he comes back to Grandma's for dinner," Tamsin said worriedly.

"I think he will," Justin said. "I think he probably just needed a little fortification after church. He was obviously uncomfortable. I think it was having to wear that jacket. I got the feeling he thought he didn't deserve to be wearing a suit jacket. He doesn't seem to have any self-confidence."

Justin was probably right, Gincy thought. Tommy had probably gone somewhere with that other man for a drink; with the bars closed for Christmas, maybe they had gone to Tommy's apartment for a few beers. But as far as she knew Tommy had never been drunk in his mother's presence. She wasn't worried that he would show up at the house in a sorry state.

As for Tommy lacking self-confidence, well, sadly, Justin was right about that, as well.

"I hope he comes back, too," she said. "I'm making creamed onions. They're his favorite. Even when he was a little kid he loved creamed onions. It's not something most kids like."

Rick turned to smile at his wife.

"Keep your eyes on the road, Richard."

"Mom," Tamsin said, "don't forget about the roof. We have to check Grandma's roof."

"What's wrong with it?" Justin asked.

"We don't know," Gincy told him. "Maybe nothing, but it's on the to-do list."

"Well, we'd better get moving on that," Justin said. "There's a big snowstorm predicted for the middle of next week. I'll check Grandpa's notes for the phone number of his repair guys and make a call first thing tomorrow."

Gincy looked over her shoulder at her stepson. "Thank you, Justin," she said. "That would be a huge help. By the way, Tamsin told us that you and the—that you and Lisa—broke up."

"Yeah. She wanted a commitment from me I just wasn't ready to give." Justin laughed. "But her heart's not broken. She's already seeing someone else."

"That's good," Tamsin said. "I mean that her heart's not broken."

"Besides, that nose ring was beginning to gross me out."

Gincy hooted with laughter. "I knew it!" she cried.

"Septum piercing, Justin," Tamsin said primly.

A few minutes later the family pulled up at Number Nineteen Crescent Road to see Tommy just getting out of his mother's car. He was wearing the coat Rick had passed on to him, and Gincy could see that underneath it he wore only a T-shirt. The old suit jacket had been abandoned somewhere along the line.

"He's home already!" Tamsin cried. "I'm so glad!"

Gincy smiled. "Me too," she said. She felt very, very lucky at that moment to have all that she had. Mom and Tommy. Rick and Justin and Tamsin. Danielle and Clare. The memory of her father. A surfeit of riches.

There was no doubt about it, she thought, getting out of the car and waving to her brother, who waved back to her. The best Christmas present you could ever give or receive was love.

And it cost so very little.

Please read on
for a very special Q&A
with Holly Chamberlin!

This novel reintroduces characters we met in *The Summer of Us*, first published in 2004. Why did you choose to revisit Gincy, Danielle, and Clare all these years later?

The first reason I brought back the three characters I created all those years ago is that I sincerely liked them. For some reason I especially took to Gincy Gannon, so she was the obvious lead character for this current novel. The second reason is that so many readers have requested a sequel to *The Summer of Us* that it was a pleasure to finally be able to oblige. Many readers would also like to meet the characters from *The Family Beach House* again, and I would love to revisit the McQueen family, too!

Gincy and her friends are now closing in on fifty years of age, with husbands and children. Was it a challenge to age them from the thirty-year-olds they were in *The Summer of Us*?

Honestly, not really, because I've aged right along with my characters! At fifty-two I'm definitely not who I was at thirty or even at forty. I mean, I'm not unrecognizable to friends and family, but I've certainly changed, we all do, and hopefully, though not always, for the better.

In *The Season of Us* we see a strong and comfortable relationship between grandparents and grandchildren. Is this something you experienced in your own life?

It is. My brother and I were extremely lucky to live in near proximity to my mother's parents. We all met regularly for family dinners and, of course, for the holidays, and on occasion my brother and I would spend the night at Grandma and Grandpa's apartment. They had very little money, but treated us so nicely with trips to an old-fashioned ice-cream parlor (long since gone, sadly), visits to the playground, and longs walks through the city. And my grandmother made the best roast beef *ever*. For a while I sang in a folk group for which my grandfather was the drummer! And when Grandpa had his stroke—the first of several—my brother, being a big guy as well, was so helpful with his care. If you're lucky enough to have grandparents in your life, appreciate it!

What are some of your most vivid memories of Christmas as a child?

I have so many incredibly vivid memories I hardly know where to begin, but I'll start with the obvious—books. Each year I would get a hardcover novel from my parents and I'd sit in the armchair right next to the tree (always a real one with a lovely pine smell) and read for hours. One year it was *Gone with the Wind*. Another year it was *Eight Cousins* by Louisa May Alcott. I also remember these yummy German spice cookies my mother would put in our stockings; they were iced and had a vintage image of Santa Claus sort of pasted onto the icing. It was impossible to get the image off cleanly, so you always wound up eating some of it along with the cookie!

What stands out from the more recent Christmases you've celebrated?

When we lived in Cape Neddick we opened the front door one morning a few days before Christmas to find this utterly creepy and fantastic candleholder/sculpture thingie featuring an elfish sort of being with a maniacal expression on his face reminiscent of Pee-wee Herman. We were at a complete loss as to how it got there and who left it. All of our local friends roundly denied being responsible, and I was tearing my hair out until our very funny neighbor, Sue, finally confessed. She knew I loved Pee-wee Herman and when she saw this crazy thing that looked like a cross between Pee-wee and an evil circus character, she couldn't resist! Every year he has pride of place in our house.

THE SEASON
OF US

Holly Chamberlin

ABOUT THIS GUIDE

The suggested questions are included to enhance
your group's reading of Holly Chamberlin's
The Season of Us!

Discussion Questions

1. Above all, be kind. This is the message that Gincy tries to keep in mind when dealing with others, especially those with whom she has a strained relationship. How important is basic kindness, really? Do you believe that small acts of kindness can effect big change?

2. Clare, Gincy, and Tamsin talk about needing perspective and "a breath of fresh air" when dealing with family members, particularly those who can be difficult. Talk about how the weight of one's experience with family can sometimes crush better feelings and tendencies toward love and forgiveness.

3. Gincy looks at her forty-five-year-old brother, by society's standards a failure, and remembers him as a child, vulnerable, blameless, and full of promise. Could Gincy have been right to some extent when she accused her parents, especially her mother, of being an enabler, of not pushing Tommy to succeed? Do you think the Gannons' policy of acceptance concerning their son was the wisest choice? How does a person know how and when to limit their expectations of a loved one and simply make peace with him?

4. Keeping in touch with friends, especially those who are far flung, can be a real challenge. It might be said that Gincy, Danielle, and Clare have achieved the ideal of active communication. Talk about your own

experiences of trying to maintain friendships through all of the changes life brings. Does social media ever replace face-to-face communication? Former generations were accustomed to having long telephone conversations with friends and family at a distance, and to exchanging lengthy handwritten letters, both of which required time, patience, and dedication. Talk about how things are different now in the age of emoticons, Facebook, and texting.

5. Ellen and Ed Gannon seemed to have chosen a largely solitary life together rather than to develop a strong circle of friends. Though a perfectly acceptable choice, talk about how/if/when it might not be the best way for a couple to face the future, especially when one spouse passes away, leaving the other behind.

6. In both novels featuring Gincy—*The Summer of Us* and *The Season of Us*—she thinks about what a person owes to family. As a thirty-year-old, she is inclined to look away from those family members she finds difficult or disappointing, but as a fifty-year-old she realizes she is no longer able to ignore her mother and her brother. She chooses tolerance and sympathy over intolerance and judgment when dealing with them. Though there are situations in which abandoning a family member is justifiable, Gincy realizes that she is not in such a situation. What circumstances might justify a person's rejecting participation in family duty?

In a charming Maine seaside town, a single mother longs to create a memorable Christmas for her two daughters—and receives a chance to make her own wishes come true, in this heartwarming novel from bestselling author Holly Chamberlin.

At first glance, Nell King's cozy home in Yorktide, Maine, seems a step down from the impeccably decorated Boston house she shared with her husband. But in the six years since he abruptly left to marry another woman, Nell and her almost-grown daughters have found real happiness and comfort here. Now, faced with what may be their last Christmas together before Molly and Felicity move away, Nell suddenly feels anxious. She gave up her own ambitions when she married. With the daily obligations of motherhood coming to an end, what role is left for her to fill?

Twenty-one-year-old Molly has never forgiven her father for walking out, though she worries about sacrificing her independence the way her mother did. Should she stay in Maine with her dependable boyfriend, or move to the city and prove herself? Felicity, meanwhile, is torn between loyalty to Nell and wanting to spend time with her glamorous, ski champion stepmother. Nell is eager to cement the bond with her daughters by making this holiday picture-perfect. But there's a complication—and an opportunity. . . .

Nell's first and greatest love, now a successful novelist, has arrived in town for a book signing. As the two rekindle their friendship, Nell confronts the choices and compromises she once made in the name of stability. And as the coming days unfold with revelations and unexpected gifts, this Christmas promises to herald a bright new beginning.

Please keep reading for an exciting sneak peek of Holly Chamberlin's

HOME FOR CHRISTMAS

coming soon wherever print and e-books are sold!

"Our hearts grow tender with childhood memories and love of kindred, and we are better for having, in spirit, become a child again at Christmas-time."
—Laura Ingalls Wilder

CHAPTER 1

It was the eleventh of December, a crisp winter day with not a cloud in the sky to threaten rain or snow. Nell King shivered as she came down the stairs from the second floor and into the living room. It was her habit to keep the heat low during the day when she and the girls were most often out. While the habit saved money, it did mean that from about the middle of November through the end of March Nell, Molly, and Felicity went around the house bundled to the teeth. At the moment Nell was wearing a plaid flannel shirt over a thermal t-shirt, lined jeans, and wool slipper socks. Her dark hair was piled into a messy updo and her face was free of makeup.

Not that she ever wore much makeup these days. There was no need for concealment or for disguise, not in Nell's world, and though once upon a time she had taken pleasure in preening and primping, since her divorce six years earlier the idea of dressing and making up held virtually no appeal. At least she hadn't taken to wearing her pajamas and slippers out of the house. The day that happened, Nell thought, she would have let the whole casual thing go too far and would need a stylist's intervention.

With a feeling of satisfaction Nell surveyed the living room. She had begun decorating for the Christmas season immediately after Thanksgiving. No sooner had the ears of Indian corn and the oddly shaped gourds and the sprays of red, orange, and yellow leaves been tucked away than the baubles and bows of Christmas made their appearance. The windows were outlined with tiny white lights. Fresh green garland was wound around the handrail of the stairs to the second floor. A large, cut-glass bowl was filled with colorful, glossy ribbon candy. A tall glass jar held an array of candy canes. Slabs of peanut brittle were artfully arranged on a rectangular ceramic plate with a pretty green glaze. A gingerbread house had pride of place on the coffee table. It was a full two feet high and sat on a base one foot square. The roof was comprised of round red-and-white peppermint candies. The window shutters were made of sticks of gum while the windowpanes had been crafted of leaf gelatin. Red M & Ms made up the house's two chimneys, and candy canes represented lampposts. Every surface that could be was heavily covered with colored fondant and marzipan.

But the real star of the holiday season was the massive evergreen tree waiting to be decorated with ornaments that held a special meaning for Nell and her daughters. There was the set of tiny angels dressed in Victorian garb that Nell's maternal grandmother had given her shortly before she died. There were the five crystal icicles Molly had won in a raffle back in middle school. And there was the figurine of Dr. Seuss's infamous Grinch that Felicity had bought with the money she had earned from her first paying job as a delivery person for the *Yorktide Daily Chronicle.*

Seventeen-year-old Felicity's eyes had popped when she

first saw this year's tree, its long branches gracefully spreading from its sturdy trunk. "This is the biggest tree we've ever had," she had said. "How did you get it through the front door?"

Nell had smiled enigmatically; in fact she had hired two young workers at the Christmas tree lot to deliver the tree and wrangle it into its stand, a new one Nell had purchased as the one she already owned was far too small for the trunk of this giant.

But one Christmas tree wasn't enough, not this year. A small artificial tree stood on a table on the landing of the second floor; it was hung with skeletons of starfish; seashells of various shapes and sizes; bits of green and blue sea glass; plastic lobsters; little wooden lobster traps; and a selection of ceramic moose, loons, puffins and bears.

"Uh, Mom," twenty-one-year-old Molly had said when Nell had been putting the final touches on the tree. "We know we live in Maine. We know we might run across a moose on the road at any time, though I seriously hope we don't."

"What's your point?" Nell had asked.

"It's just that a tree like this should be in the lobby of a hotel or a retail store. It's like an advertisement."

Nell's disappointment must have shown on her face because Molly had immediately added: "Sorry, Mom. I wasn't criticizing, really."

Another small tree stood on a sideboard in the dining room, this one decorated with ornaments related to Santa Claus in his various guises, from the stately and solemn St. Nicholas, secret gift-giver and patron saint of sailors; to the uniquely English versions of Father Christmas, clutching wassail bowls and dressed in furred and hooded gowns, with wreaths of holly encircling their heads; to the jolly, bearded American Santa of *Rudolph the Red-Nosed Reindeer* fame, with red suit trimmed in white fur, black boots and belt, and a hat tipped with a white fur pom-pom. This was the Santa Claus to be found in every mall in the United States from just after Thanksgiving until Christmas Eve, the Santa Claus who posed for pictures with small, often bewildered children perched on his lap. It was a matter of regret for Nell that she had never managed to get such a portrait of the girls with Santa. It hadn't been for lack of trying. Sheer bad luck had gotten in the way.

Nell had decorated the girls' bedrooms for the holidays, too, though with more restraint than she had employed with the rest of the house; she respected their rooms as private spaces, so she had confined herself to hanging a jingle bell from each doorknob and a fabric wall hanging on the back of each closet door.

As for Nell's own bedroom, well, it was empty of anything relating to Christmas other than the materials for the secret craft projects on which she was working. It simply hadn't seemed worth the effort to add a jingle bell or a wall hanging for her own enjoyment. And her daughters wouldn't notice; it had been years since either girl had come to her mother's room to cuddle with her in the new bed Nell had bought when they first moved to Yorktide. Her old bed, the one she had shared for more than fifteen years with Joel, had swiftly gone to a charity shop. Nell did not hate her ex-husband in spite of the fact that he had left her for his mistress, but neither did she need so solid a reminder of their past intimate life in her new home.

Nell continued on to the kitchen now, where the large square table was set up for the day's craft project. She took a seat, and as she did so she was suddenly overwhelmed by a sense of sadness tinged with bittersweet nostalgia. It wasn't the first time this season she had been overcome with these feelings, and she knew it would not be the last, for this Christmas might very well be the final one she would spend with both of her children under one roof. By this time the following year Nell thought it was likely that Molly would be married or at least engaged to Mick Williams, her longtime boyfriend, and as for Felicity . . .

The news had come as a very great shock. Felicity had spent the weekend after Thanksgiving in Boston with her father and stepmother and Pam's eight-year-old son, Taylor. On Sunday evening Nell met Felicity at the bus station at the old Pease Air Force Base off the turnpike in Portsmouth, and no sooner had Felicity slid into the passenger seat of Nell's serviceable Subaru than she had dropped her bombshell. "Dad and Pam have invited me to join them in Switzerland next Christmas! We'll be staying at a swanky ski lodge, and they're paying for everything, including my airfare. Isn't that fantastic? I can't wait for next year. I am so excited."

Nell had started the engine and steered the car out of the station. "Didn't you think to check with me first?" she asked as casually as she could manage, which wasn't very casually at all. Her heart was hurting.

"No," Felicity had replied promptly. "Why? Anyway, I am so looking forward to next year!"

"What about this Christmas?" Nell had asked, ignoring her daughter's unconsciously callous reply. "Aren't you looking forward to this Christmas with your sister and me at home in Maine?"

Felicity had shrugged. "Yeah. But Europe, Mom! That's so much cooler. Who knows what sort of interesting people I might meet? Maybe even some gorgeous Italian guys. Let's face it, I know just about everybody in Yorktide by name and absolutely *everybody* by sight. Nothing new or exciting ever happens here. Boring!"

Well, Nell supposed Yorktide would seem boring to a young woman of Felicity's vibrant and outgoing personality. Still, Felicity had never expressed boredom with her home before, not until her stepmother had filled her head with visions of exotic places peopled by immoral millionaires and overrated actors and who knew what other dubious types!

Nell took a deep and calming breath, picked up the container of Elmer's glue, and attempted to concentrate on the task at hand. It was not easy to do. Since Felicity's momentous announcement Nell had been fixated on the fact that both of her children would soon be leaving home, and the idea filled her with dread. Next August Felicity would be a freshman at the University of Michigan in Ann Arbor. And while it was true that Molly would still be local after her marriage to Mick, whenever exactly that took place, she would have her own life to live, a husband and in-laws and, sooner rather than later, children for whom to care. Add to that the duties demanded of Molly as a farmer's wife, including her continuing involvement with the Maine Farm Bureau, where Mick was a member of the Young Farmer and Rancher Committee, and there was little doubt in Nell's mind that even at the best of times she would see her older daughter only once or twice a week.

The house on Trinity Lane, the cozy and charming house in which Nell and her daughters had lived happily for the past six years, would feel horribly empty before long. It had been a risk to relocate the girls from Drayton, Massachusetts, to Yorktide, where they knew absolutely no one, but it had been important to Nell to remove her children from their stepmother's immediate influence. Pam Bertrand-King, Olympic gold medalist in skiing, often featured in the pages of the glossy magazines Felicity enjoyed, the face of high-end car companies and manufacturers of athletic clothing and trendy new jewelry designers. Molly and Felicity had indeed been upset about leaving old friends, but soon enough they had made new friends and found a warm welcome in southern Maine.

All three of the King women had fallen immediately in love with the classic white clapboard farmhouse, and Nell had set about decorating it to reflect *her* personality rather than her mother's. It was Jacqueline Emerson who had dictated the decorating of the house her daughter and son-in-law had moved into twenty-some-odd years earlier. Here, structured sofas had been replaced with comfy couches. Hard edges and clean lines had been left behind in favor of rounded corners and curves. A neutral palette of taupe, tan, and black had been rejected in favor of warm and vibrant pinks, reds, and greens. Flowers fresh from the garden arranged naturally in a milk jug had taken the place of a formal arrangement purchased weekly from a select florist. This house in Yorktide felt to Nell so much more *livable* than had the house back in Drayton.

Suddenly, Nell heard the front door open, followed by Felicity's distinctive lilting laugh and Molly's more subdued, serious tone. A moment or two later the girls came into the kitchen.

Molly was tall and athletically built, much like her father, something that had upset her for about a minute when at the age of twelve she was larger than most of her classmates. She had endured some teasing from boys and girls alike, but she had come through the difficult experience beautifully. That was Molly. She was never shaken for long. This afternoon she was wearing her favorite pair of eyeglasses, square, dark tortoiseshell frames.

Unlike her sister, Felicity was petite. Her long, dark brown hair was pulled into a high ponytail, a ponytail that tended to swing wildly when she strode through a room or bounded up a flight of stairs. Both girls were dressed in ubiquitous cold weather gear—puffer coats, lined leggings, boots from L. L. Bean, and super long wool scarves wound several times around their necks.

"Hey, Mom," Felicity said, giving her mother a kiss on the cheek. "What's all this?"

Nell smiled. "I'm making toy soldiers and snowmen."

"Since when have you been so into crafts?" Molly asked. "You've been working away at some project or another every day for weeks."

"I've always liked doing crafts," Nell protested.

"No you haven't," Molly countered, "except for the time you took that pottery class."

Felicity laughed. "No offense, Mom, but that jug you made was pretty awful. It didn't pour right and the color was really icky."

Nell shrugged. "Pottery just wasn't my thing."

"And making toy soldiers out of gum drops and snowmen out of marshmallows is your thing?" Molly asked, taking a green gumdrop from the pile on the table and popping it into her mouth.

"You have to admit it's a cute idea," Nell protested. "I found it in a Christmas craft book I got at the library."

"But what are we supposed to *do* with them?" Molly asked.

"Well, you anchor the supporting stick of each figure into a white Styrofoam block and then you have a row of soldiers and snowmen standing in the snow," Nell explained. "The Styrofoam represents the snow."

Molly raised an eyebrow. "If you say so." Her cell phone rang; she pulled it from her pocket and frowned at the screen.

"Who is it?" Nell asked.

"Mick. I'll call him back later."

For a brief moment Nell wondered why Molly had frowned. Maybe Molly had had a spat with Mick, though Mick was so good-natured Nell found it hard to imagine anyone being out of sorts with him for long. Mick had graduated college two years earlier with a degree in agricultural studies and had sound plans for expanding his family's farm. A young woman could do an awful lot worse than to marry Mick Williams.

"Do you want me to handle dinner, Mom?" Molly asked. "I could make hamburgers."

"That's okay," Nell replied. "I've got dinner planned."

"Then I'm going to take a hot shower," Molly announced. "I can't seem to shake this chill I got when I stopped to help Mr. Milton change a tire."

"And I need to start my math homework," Felicity added. "I hate trigonometry. I don't know why I have to take it when there's no way I'm going to ever use it."

When both girls had gone upstairs and Nell was sitting alone in the midst of half-constructed candy soldiers and marshmallow snowmen, she felt that too familiar wave of sadness wash over her again. She thought about the pinecones she had covered in silver-and-gold glitter; the fat pillar candles around which she had wrapped bright red ribbon; the tree-shaped napkin rings she had made out of construction paper; the place cards in the shape of holly leaves; the red and white poinsettia plants she had arranged in groups around the house. Christmas crafts, no matter how beautiful or charming, weren't going to stop the inevitable from happening. Nell knew that. And yet she continued to squeeze glue and sprinkle glitter and wield knitting needles in some vain and vaguely superstitious attempt to keep her children where they belonged. At home with their mother.